The

Iain Thompson

Copyright © Iain Thompson (2021)

No part of this publication may be reproduced by any means, including photocopying, recording, electronic, mechanical or otherwise without prior permission of the Author and copyright owner.

All rights reserved.

This book is a work of fiction.

All characters in this publication, other than the obvious historical characters, are fictitious and any resemblance to actual persons, living or dead, is purely coincidental.

This book is transcribed using conventional (British) English. Therefore, some classical Greek words, names and phrases have been adapted purely for the purpose of this book.

ISBN: 9798708155238

Independently Published.

For my children Ivy, Maisie & Betty

My entire world

CHARACTER LIST

The character names marked with a * are based on historical figures. The remaining names are fictional characters, some of which may be influenced by other historical figures.

*Anaxandridas II - Agiad King of Sparta
*Cleomenes - The eldest son of King Anaxandridas (2nd wife).
*Dorieus – The second son of King Anaxandridas (1st wife).
*Leonidas – Son of Anaxandridas (1st wife)
*Cleombrotus – Twin brother to Leonidas.
*Gorgo – Daughter to Cleomenes and wife to Leonidas.
*Demaratus – Eurypontid King of Sparta
*Isagoras – Athenian Aristocrat
*Cleisthenes – Opposed Athenian Aristocrat
*Leotychidas – Eurypontid King of Sparta
*Xerxes – King of Persia
*Pleistarchus – Son of Leonidas
*Themistocles – Athenian Politician and General
*Aristodemus – A Spartan Soldier/Officer
*Eurytus – A Spartan Soldier
*Demophilus – Thespian Commander
*Hydarnes – Persian Commander
*Ephialtes – Traitor
*Abrocomes – Brother of King Xerxes
*Hyperanthes – Brother of King Xerxes
*Tyrrhastiadas – Persian Captain, Noble and Messenger
*The Delphic Oracle/Pythian Priestess
Brelos – Servant to King Anaxandridas.
Cora – Wife of Isagoras
Tiro – A Spartan Soldier and Polemarch
Orien – A Greek
Aglea – A Greek
Agis – A Spartan
Adonis – Messene farmer

Cicero – An Ephor
Rhea – Cicero's wife
Alec – A Spartan Soldier
Lycurgus – Spartan Elder
Savrellos – Helot
Theodore – Locrian Farmer
Calisto – Theodore's wife

PROLOGUE

540 BC, Greece has suffered generations of war, its political noblemen are rife with corruption and Athens is at the helm. With limitless power it leaves the rest of Greece in fear of further war, poverty and slavery. Except one city, Sparta.

For hundreds of years the city-state of Sparta has rules outside of Athens reach, that have previously been the cause of many conflicts. Sparta's leaders and political powers take pride in their customs and stubbornness to obey any other state, no matter the cost.

Ruled by two Kings simultaneously of the Agiad and Eurypontid dynasties, from the lineage of twins Eurysthenes and Procles, descendants of Heracles, who conquered Sparta after the Trojan wars.

However, there is one man who quietly doubts his city's limits and what place Sparta will have in Greece in the coming years, and whether his heirs are up to the challenge, King Anaxandridas II of the Agiad dynasty.

The King needed male heirs and to the Ephors dissatisfaction, the first wife was barren. The five Ephors, the administrators of Sparta, allowed permission for a second wife. The Ephors were mistaken and impatient as both Queens gave birth to a son.

His first wife had a son named Dorieus, but his second wife gave birth first to their son, Cleomenes.

Several years later, the King approaches the Queen from behind, placing his hands on her shoulders; she is the first wife and is expecting their second child to arrive into the world, currently overdue.

She notices the pressures of being one of the Spartan Kings through his glazed eyes. His skin is dry and his hair is long, his beard untrimmed for some time. The King looks more tired than usual, weighed down with his responsibilities. Keeping his thoughts to himself, the King has concerns for his new child and hopes Sparta's traditions prevail over the odds. Although their new child will not be the heir to his crown, he gazes out over the roof tops of the city, curious to what the Oracle would have to say. A visit long overdue.

Night is falling and the moon is already visible and bright. A fine mist is moving through the streets of Sparta while the King walks alone in its shadows, breaking the mist and its fluidity as he walks through, making his journey to the Oracle, the Pythian Priestess, the most authoritative Oracle in all of Greece.

The Oracle lived outside the city limits on Mount Parnassus, Delphi. Despite looking poverty stricken, the Oracle is not short of wealth and is thought to be heavily corrupt and powerful. However, the King feels obliged to visit and persists with his ascent.

A long climb to the Oracle situates the King high above Delphi. By this point darkness has fallen and Sparta is no longer in sight, hiding the putrid smell of Helot slaves that wonder the streets serving the Spartans. They search for scraps of food, or if they are brave enough, look to steal it, instant death if caught.

The Oracle welcomes the King, as if she was expecting his unplanned visit. The King offers fresh food and grain, coin has no place here. However, a gift of gold is welcomed.

Without delay the Oracle sits up and as if like magic a mysterious yellow mist appears before her that she seems to embrace, inhaling it deeply. The King keeps his distance, he can taste the yellow mist that surrounds him, leaving his mouth dry and his nostrils stinging.

She informs the King of change, as if the grain and fresh food suddenly allows her visions to appear clear before her. She mutters incomprehensible words, the King moves forward to make sense of what is being said, '*A waste of time!*' the King thinks to himself.

The Oracle Stops for a moment, her eyes wide open and bloodshot, gazing at a vision before her very eyes.

'A new King from two will rise and become eternal in the name of Sparta, but not before corruption, betrayal and murder.'

As usual, her visions meant nothing at first to the King as he already has heirs that will take his place. Feeling unsatisfied, he curses the Oracle and leaves promptly.
'I'd get more sense from the Gods than the Oracle,' the King mumbles to himself, looking to the sky.
Finally, returning to his residents, he hears a faint groan from within the house. Brelos runs out to greet him, a servant who serves the house of Agiad and is considered a free man who stays and serves the King by his own free will.
'Please, Sir, follow me, the Queen is about to give birth!'
The King rushes inside to see the head of his new child crowning. His Queen is pale, silent with focus, her hair wet from the efforts of labor, as she is guided through the birth.
The King waits out of sight while his Queen is seen to; suddenly, the cries and screaming of a child are travelling through the house. As the King enters the room he stops, one of the Queen's Helot slaves helping to deliver the baby approaches the King. Not being allowed to look at him in the eyes she says, 'May the God's bless your children with health and strength.'
'Children, you say?' the King thought to himself.
As he pulled back the blood-stained silk curtain that partially draped over his Queen, he was presented with twin boys.
The staff cared for the babies until the next morning, the sunlight was strong and already the hot stench of Sparta's streets filled the air.
It is customary in Sparta that newborns are inspected for any abnormalities and weaknesses, this is a city-state affair and parents have no influence over the decision.
The King can hear the soldier's footsteps cross his courtyard to collect the children, for inspection by the Gerousia.
The Gerousia was a Spartan council of elders, consisting of thirty men, of whom twenty-eight had to be over the age of sixty. Two major roles of the Gerousia were to debate motions

that were to be put before the citizen assembly. Secondly, it functioned as a supreme court, with the right to try any Spartan, up to and including the Kings. It was a powerful council that could overturn any decision, even a decision made by the Spartan assembly.

There was no anticipation between the King and Queen, Spartan law was harsh and uncompromising, making them cold to the fact their children may be left on Mount Taygetus to die or be salvaged and raised by Helot slaves.

Both children are later returned to the quarters, passing the ruthless inspection. That evening, one of the children cries out and screams with nobody to attend the child. Even as early as this, they are expected to not fear the dark and are left in solitude.

'Morning Sir, the Gods bless us with another fine day,' greeted Brelos, as he swept through the courtyard.

'Brelos,' the King replied in a slightly uninterested response.

'Forgive me for asking Sir, it's not my place, but have you named the children?'

Brelos was one of few people that could get away with asking such questions, it was known for the King to sometimes ask for his advice and opinions. Although a former slave to the Athenians, Brelos had a good knowledge of economics, politics and warfare and was widely trusted throughout the household.

'Yes!' the King said, excited to inform Brelos of the news. 'Come this way Brelos, let me introduce you to the future of Sparta.' Leading him back through the house to the nursing quarters. 'This is Cleombrotus, he was the second one to arrive and the noisiest by all accounts, a weakness to become strength, I hope Brelos.'

'I'm sure of it, Sir. And this one?'

The King pauses for just a moment, a moment long enough to recall his visit to the Oracle. *'A new King will rise from two,'* he thought to himself.

As the King reached in to raise the child from his bedding, a strange feeling overwhelmed him, one he has not felt before.

He gazed deep into the eyes that innocently gazed back, he could smell the sweet wine used to bathe the child still on his perfect skin. The King was in a state of daydream, he could feel the breeze, rolling off the Aegean Sea and gently caressing the back of his neck.

The King seemed relaxed, forgetting all his previous political worries and duties while embracing the child. At that moment, the pressure of being King seemed to fade.

'Sir, is everything ok?'

'Yes, it is Brelos,' he says, breaking eye contact briefly with the child. *'His name.'* The King thought for a moment with a pause, gazing back in to the large, uncorrupt, brown eyes.

'His name is Leonidas.'

1

Six years later, Sparta has continued to grow from strength to strength. The streets are dusty, overcrowded and hot with market stands, making a roaring trade. You can't help but notice the smell of fruits, fish and herbs as you pass through the markets before suddenly, overwhelmed by the stench of a passing donkey or Helot slave, moving produce for their masters.

Leonidas knows the streets well and spends much of his free time along the banks of the Eurotus River, one of his favorite locations to play. Leonidas has a sense of free will, probably more so than his elder brothers. The chances of Leonidas inheriting the title of the King of Sparta are zero to none; he is not considered an heir to the throne.

However, in the back of his mind he is more than aware his seventh birthday is approaching, this means only one thing for a male Spartan, the Agoge.

Leonidas was considered a Prince that was not inline to the throne; therefore, the Agoge would be expecting his arrival. His primary role, along with so many other Spartan boys, was to be a Soldier, a warrior of war.

The Agoge is a compulsory state sponsored education system, it is a place where children must enter and endure a life of hardship, discipline, pain and constant training to become the best warriors Sparta can produce. Above violence, they are taught that loyalty to the state comes first, before their own needs and even before their own families.

The Helot slaves played an important part in this system, they were the fellow Greeks who would handle all day-to-day labour, in order to keep the Spartan society functioning properly.

The day was closing in, Leonidas had made his way home, his mother sat patiently for him on a fountain wall, within their courtyard. As Leonidas entered, his Father was returning home from his duties.

'Those Fucking Athenians have a lot to answer for!' the King shouts, pacing his way through the yard. It was rare to hear the King curse out loud, he was always so composed.

The King came to an abrupt halt, he had noticed his Queen and Leonidas sat by the fountain. The King had a soft spot for Leonidas, but did not dare show it as this is seen as a sign of weakness, especially when Leonidas is due to enter the Agoge.

Entering the Agoge has been playing on the mind of Leonidas, curiosity more than anything else. Horror stories always seemed to seep out from the Agoge, and it wouldn't take long for Leonidas to hear them.

'What is heavy on your mind Leonidas?' the King asks, catching Leonidas off guard, as if reading his mind.

'Curiosity and anxiety taunt my mind, while I wait to be taken to the Agoge,' replies Leonidas, with a concerned look on his face.

Suddenly, the King back hands Leonidas across the face, sending him crashing into the sand.

'You dare speak such negativity before me child, you will not shame the house of Agiad!' the King yells, before turning sharply in the sand and walking off.

Leonidas, still on the floor, turns over onto his back gazing up at his Mother, expecting a level of sympathy or calming words. The Queen says nothing, she calmly stands and proceeds to follow her King.

His lip bleeds slightly as he spits blood and sand from his mouth. *'My Father must be under a great deal of pressure from the council,'* Leonidas thinks to himself, trying to justify the King's response. As he stands, he washes his face in the fountain, pausing to stare at his reflection.

As Leonidas looks up, he glances through the pillars surrounding the courtyard; they are already casting large shadows as they fall into darkness. A face attracts Leonidas's attention, in what little light remains.

'Brelos, is that you?' Leonidas asks, wondering how long he has been stood there for.

Brelos says nothing, and returns to his tasks. It did seem slightly strange to Leonidas that Brelos would be watching, but knew that any interruption or unwanted presence could get him a serious beating, slave or not.

The night was cooler than normal, there was a breeze that kept interrupting Leonidas's sleep. His body was tired, but his mind was wide awake, his seventh birthday was only a matter of days away, too many questions entered his mind.

'How will I manage in the Agoge?' the not knowing bothered Leonidas, he wished he had the authority to speak to the Oracle for guidance. *'Will I do Sparta and my family proud, and will I see war?'* as he questioned his own abilities, Leonidas gradually settled into a deep sleep.

With each closing day, Leonidas knew the inevitable would happen. A new morning had arrived, the sun was sitting low and bright, cascading through the doorway leading into where Leonidas lay. Leonidas lay still, partly awake embracing the warmth of the sun on his face. Suddenly, his skin felt cold and the light had faded.

'Sir, forgive me for waking you, but the King has asked for your company at his quarters,' Brelos says, leaning over Leonidas, he moves back to allow him to get up.

'Regarding what, Brelos?' he replies, shading his squinting eyes from the morning sun.

'I don't know, Sir, that wouldn't be my place to ask, but it sounds important.' Brelos bows, then leaves Leonidas.

'Very well,' replies Leonidas, by which point Brelos had left the room. Leonidas gathers himself together, then makes his way to his Father's quarters, where he waits with his brother, Cleombrotus.

'Sit,' the King demanded. 'I will keep this brief, as you know what is expected of you both. You are both turning of age in two days and you will be collected to start your education, understood?'

'Yes Father,' both answering, almost perfectly in sync.

'Good, off you go,' the King kept things brief, the need for further conversation was not necessary.

'Are you scared Brother?' Cleombrotus asks, shoving Leonidas from behind. Cleombrotus was always the bigger built of the two and appeared to have more self-confidence.

'Of course, I am not, you Ass!' Feeling insulted, Leonidas storms off ignoring his brother.

Leonidas and Cleombrotus were born many years after their two elder brothers; their half-brother, Cleomenes, already had a daughter called Gorgo. Rumours spread around Sparta quickly about their birth being a burden and how they were not really considered as Spartan Princes. Even rumours about their own Mother not wanting them, were travelling in whispers around Sparta.

However, they were the same age and were about to start the Agoge training together. Close or not, they will experience a whole new way of life.

Several days have passed, the twins have had their seventh birthday, there are no celebrations.

Brelos enters the room where Leonidas and Cleombrotus are sat. No words are spoken as the twins know why he has come. Brelos confirms their thoughts with a single nod of his head.

Leonidas and Cleombrotus stand up with no hesitation, they know what is expected of them and they walk to the front of the house, where the King and Queen both wait.

Despite the rumors, the Queen hides her emotions well and kisses each of them goodbye. Leonidas looks up to his Father, standing in his shadow, as the King towers over him.

The King places a hand on the shoulder of Leonidas, squeezing it gently, he says nothing. Leonidas knows the grasp on his shoulder are the words his Father won't speak '*Goodbye Son.*' Brelos opens the door, releasing an intense burst of sunlight; a gentle wind lifts the sands from the floor, creating a swirling cloud in the air, followed by the fallen leaves before settling to the ground. Breaking the sunlight, two soldiers stand in the doorway creating a silhouette, their long red cloaks flap in the breeze, while the sunlight beams off their armour. They both greet the King and Queen accordingly and encourage the twins to move along. Leonidas and Cleombrotus make their way to the transport that waits; a beautiful strong looking horse stands before them, with a cart.

They pass the horse and step up into the cart, lending each other a supporting hand. *'Even the horse looks like he knows what we are getting in to,'* thought Leonidas. As they both turn to say a final farewell to their parents, the King and Queen have already turned away, and Brelos is closing the doors. 'This is it Leonidas!' Cleombrotus says in a slightly nervous, excited manner, 'we are soldiers of Sparta now Leonidas.'

'Not yet prince,' replied one of the soldiers from the front, laughing hysterically.

The journey to the Agoge was long, rough, hot and uncomfortable. Suddenly, through the hot haze rising from the sands, a mirage of the Agoge appears.

'It's larger than I imagined,' Leonidas says to Cleombrotus, as they approach the bleak looking, heavily guarded barracks.

The first thing Leonidas immediately noticed was the overwhelming smell; he couldn't quite put his finger on it at first. As they were led towards the entrance, the gate opened with no command given and the smell Leonidas noticed before became incredibly strong, followed by an outcry of noise, crashing and yelling and the distinctive sound, the crack of a whip.

Leonidas turns to Cleombrotus. 'You do not seem so talkative now, brother.'

'You want to talk, brother?' Cleombrotus replies, rather surprisingly. The center of the Agoge is a vast dusty space, a hive of activity. Spartan boys no older than Leonidas and Cleombrotus, wrestle each other to the ground before one violently slams his fist into the others face, splitting the bridge of his nose. The boy has an expression of being possessed, focused on nothing other than burying his opponents head into the ground, with only his fists. Across the way, a group of five Spartan boys armed with a wooden sword and shield surround a single, unarmed boy; with no command given, he is brutally attacked and beaten. Suddenly, in the clouds of dust, almost hidden from sight, an armed Spartan boy hits the floor hard, and then another and another, until the boy stands alone, victorious. 'Good! Extra rations for you, boy!' The instructor praises, enthusiastically.

'Thirty more!' Bellows a voice from across the training area, followed with a thunderous clap. Leonidas and Cleombrotus turn to see a young boy hanging by his wrists, while he takes lash after lash of a whip. The boys head is still held up, he makes no sound of a whimper as the whip connects with his back, each crack of the whip leaving a slice through his flesh, bloody, bruised and swollen. Between the fresh wounds, old scars are visible from previous lashings.

'Why is he being whipped?' Leonidas asks, with a cringed expression.'

'It's his punishment, for getting caught!' 'Twice in as many weeks, he shall be sold after his punishment!' The guard sniggered.

'Caught, doing what?' a curious Cleombrotus asks.

'Stealing, now move along, boy!'

It is customary in Spartan training to encourage Spartan boys to steal and take what they need to survive on their own, but if caught, they risk being sold. Despite their extremely harsh and violent training regime, they were also taught to write poetry, read and taught stealth, athletics and hunting.

Leonidas and Cleombrotus were ushered into a small holding area by one of the instructors. 'Remove all of your clothing and belongings, boys, now!' - the overseer demanded, as if he had better places to be - 'Here put these on.' Throwing clothing at them to wear.

'Smells like a hundred slaves have worn this,' Cleombrotus says, with a frown.

Leonidas looks down at his feet, before asking the overseer, a voice interrupts his thoughts. 'I'm afraid it's barefoot at best, boy! In here, privileged, you are not! Hurry along. This way,' the overseer says, followed by a smack across the head of Leonidas.

Cleombrotus and Leonidas are hurried along, tripping over each other along the way. They are halted at an old wooden door that has half its boards missing.

'In there you two, find a space and make a bed from whatever you can find.'

As they walk in the overseer pushes Cleombrotus in with his foot against his back, grabbing Leonidas around the back of his neck, he forces him in next. The dorm was cramped and crowded with odd bits of material that has been scavenged to make beds, the stale smell of sweat and the lack of ventilation was obvious.

Although the brothers had not been pampered during their upbringing, this was still a huge culture shock and a change that would take some time to adapt to.

Dong, Dong, Dong. The sound that meant it was time to eat.

The overseer could be heard outside shouting commands at everyone to clean up and get something to eat, before the next training regime started.

Suddenly, the dorm door bursts open, spewing a cloud of dust through the room causing Leonidas and Cleombrotus to squint and cough, followed by the recruits as they rush to drop off their training aids and collect their meal. As the recruits turn to head back out the dorm, they squabble and push in front of each other hoping one can get their meal faster than the other.

Leonidas allows Cleombrotus to walk ahead, as they follow on behind, Cleombrotus looks back and smirks at Leonidas, *'uncivilized animals,'* thought Cleombrotus.

'Where do you think you are going?!' A voice shouts, as it echoes through the dorm. Cleombrotus and Leonidas stop and observe one of the Spartan recruits, pushing his way towards them. He stopped directly in front of Cleombrotus, close enough where you could smell the scent on his breath and the sweat that still wept from his pores. He was a muscular individual, who was clearly seen as a leader within the dorm, his fellow recruits gathered around him, muttering quietly, as if hoping for a fight.

'You think you deserve a meal?' the Spartan boy asks, through gritted teeth.

Glancing at Leonidas over the shoulder of Cleombrotus, making him aware the question is for him also. The Spartan boy does not even blink, as he waits for a response, starring deep into the eyes of Cleombrotus. Leonidas noticed the veins on the boy's arms, swelling as he started to clench his fists. He moved forward one step to encourage a response, startling Cleombrotus.

Cleombrotus turns to Leonidas, knowing what Cleombrotus is about to do, Leonidas takes a lung full of air, puffing his chest out. As Cleombrotus is turning back to face the boy he is greeted with a fist, connecting perfectly on the bridge of his nose, *Crunch!* Cleombrotus yelps, his legs buckle as the blood from his nose sprays over the face of Leonidas.

Leonidas dives forward to catch Cleombrotus. They both crash to the floor. The boy and his followers kick them both while they lay on the floor.

Overwhelmed and outnumbered, they cover themselves from the fists and feet that punish them.

Leonidas looks up through a gap during the short intervals between the beatings, noticing the overseer standing in the doorway, arms crossed and wearing a huge grin.

'Oi, Spartans!' the overseer bellows, in his deep voice. 'Finished tickling each other?' he sarcastically asks, followed by a laugh.

The recruits stand in an orderly line, away from Cleombrotus and Leonidas.

'Tiro, why am I not surprised it's you!' the overseer says, in an irritable tone.

'But Sir,' replies Tiro, followed by an almighty slap across his face from the overseer.

'I did not ask you for a response!' the overseer shouts, before using a nodding action to indicate the other recruits to leave.

Cleombrotus and Leonidas slowly start to help each other up to their feet, dusting themselves off.

'The three of you will take lashings for this disruption, you can find your own meals tonight!' The overseer forces them into the yard where they are told to wait until the other recruits finish their meals.

The recruits start to filter out, chanting and singing. Excitement fills the air.

Lashings were common practice in the Spartan upbringing, where they would be whipped on their backs, chest and even their faces. This was not only to teach them to embrace levels of pain, but to leave them permanently scarred to intimidate the enemy, looking battle-ridden.

However, seeing recruits whipped out of punishment made a nice change to not being whipped themselves. They all make bets on who will fall first.

The overseer pushes them over to the whipping posts where there are no ropes or chains to retain the recruits. Running would only increase the level of punishment and would not be considered an option, as the level of shame would be far worse than death itself.

'Remove your clothing!' the overseer demands. Tiro removes his clothing, bracing himself against the post, interlocking his fingers.

Cleombrotus and Leonidas do the same.

Leonidas is on the middle post, between Tiro and Cleombrotus. He looks over to Tiro, judging by the scars already on his back, he is no stranger to what he is about to go through.

The overseer rolls out his whip and looks towards the three naked recruits before him.

'Fresh meat, this may sting a little,' he says, followed by an almighty *Crack* of the whip.

Tiro takes the first lashing without as much as a whimper, barely moving from his position.

Crack, the sound of the second lashing startles Leonidas, making him whimper, despite it striking Cleombrotus.

The observing recruits laugh at the reaction of Leonidas. Leonidas looks to Cleombrotus before suddenly, an incredibly intense burning sensation is felt through his back, so intense his eyes immediately become tearful. Before Leonidas can embrace the pain, he is struck again then again and again.

By the tenth lashing, Leonidas and Cleombrotus are on their knees. Tiro remains standing; he didn't even flinch, although his eyes show he certainly felt his punishment.

Leonidas can still feel the heat through his wounds, with the cooling sensation of blood running down his back and legs. The pressure in his back increases as the wounds swell and rise up from his skin, while the breeze that passes his back, amplifies the pain.

The three of them are led away from the blood-stained sands and taken to get their wounds treated. They will not receive anything for the pain, but they will be cleaned to prevent infection. Leonidas and Cleombrotus say nothing to each other, as they try and preserve their energy. One thought crossed their mind, *'Not a good start.'*

2

Sometime has passed, and the midday heat is soaring down on Sparta and everything seems as it should be.

The markets are busy, and the city's citizens are carrying out their daily tasks. There is a sense of freedom among the Spartan citizens, their city has no walls, unheard of during this time with so many powers moving through the lands, expanding their borders.

However, this sense of freedom is not shared; especially amongst the Helot slaves, who from time to time will cause disruption within the city trying to claim back their freedom and land. At times, there can be large numbers of Helots, who in comparison massively outnumber the Spartan population and arrange sophisticated attacks; sometimes taking days to control. The sentence for such behavior will usually cost them their lives if they were to be caught. The relationship between Helots and Spartans is a bitter one, the Helot population is kept under control through strict means, but this does not stop them from planning their revolts.

There is a disturbance being noticed beyond the markets, citizens start to gather in the street to take notice. Suddenly, loud shouting can be heard and starts to get louder, followed by a group of Spartan women running the opposite way from whatever it is they see; some are also brave enough to take a stand. A small revolt has been planning an attack and has assembled to make a strong political statement, that they are free, despite being only a small number of the Helot population, they hope their protest will encourage others to join and to escalate beyond Spartan control. The Helot men storm through the street with their makeshift weapons, with some carrying swords that they have acquired or stole, causing as much destruction as they can.

A Helot slave weaves between the pillars that run parallel to the street, chasing a Spartan woman who is trying to avoid the chaos. Suddenly, she knows she can't outrun the Helot and stands her ground to fight. Spartan women are very athletic and are encouraged to take part in athletics, even learning the basics of unarmed combat.

She faces the Helot, who has an expression of desperation on his face. He looks tired and his eyes show nothing but anger as the sweat pours from his grime-stained forehead, as he raises his makeshift blade, tightly grasped in his hand.

Abruptly, the Helot's vision is compromised as the female Spartan distracts him with a piece of material that was draped around her neck. Material that was used to help keep the midday sun off of her has proven to be a valuable distraction, followed by a, *Slap*. Although slightly dazed and surprised, the Helot is fast enough to counteract by grabbing her arm and thrusting the blade straight in to her abdomen. She responds courageously, grasping his hand that holds the blade and forces it further in to her belly, spitting in his face the blood that accumulates in her mouth, before falling to her knees, dead.

Her white robe absorbs the blood before spilling on to the street and slowly flowing and seeping through the cracks in the ground. The Helot man shows no remorse, he is out to send a message that all of Sparta will fall; he disrespectfully steps over the Spartan woman and proceeds to quickly corner another.

Meanwhile, behind him, his fellow Helot slaves cause more chaos slaying anyone in their way. The streets have become stained with the blood of Spartan citizens although, some Helots have not been so lucky. Spartan citizens have outnumbered a number of them, beating them to death.

The cornered woman cries for help and fears her fate is sealed by the blade he holds, already dripping in the blood of a Spartan woman. She struggles to see the Helot man as the sun beats down, causing a strong glare off the surrounding stone walls; she accepts her fate and closes her eyes, embracing the last feeling of midday sun on her face.

She takes a lungful of air and looks up to the Gods, a gentle breeze circling her feet gently caresses her ankles, calming her sense of panic, even if only for a split second. Darkness overshadows her, and she feels the warmth of the sun fade replaced by a gentle touch of cool air.

'Am I dead?' the Spartan woman thinks to herself, too scared to attempt to open her eyes. She eventually builds the courage to slowly open her eyes; she looks down at the floor, immediately noticing the Helot man with a deep cut across his throat, from ear to ear.

The volume of blood was horrific, as it began to flow around the soles of her footwear. She noticed in front of her a composed man standing in the pool of blood, his toes and feet were black with dirt and he wore a red cloak that just about hung above the pool of blood, the ends tatty and frayed.

'A Spartan soldier, thank the Gods,' she thinks, instantly recognising their unique red cloaks.

His calf muscles were strong, and his stance was stable, holding his short sword to his side that dripped in blood from the Helot. The Spartan woman was still in shock and her senses had heightened so much so, it was as if she could hear the blood run down his sword, gently releasing off the tip making a gentle *splash* sound, as it landed in the puddle of blood below.

The sun was still cascading brightly behind the Spartan, creating a silhouette, softly highlighting features of his uniform and physique. His arms were conditioned and strong and his breast plate emphasised his build. Occasionally, sharp beams of sunlight would break through the small torn holes in his cloak, hurting her eyes, causing her to blink.

The man steps in to the sunlight, allowing her to focus on his deep green eyes that gaze through the helmet he wears. A moment of silence followed by a voice, 'Leonidas, are you done?' shouts a fellow Spartan soldier.

He turns sharply and replies, 'Yes, brother, when you deal with that on your left!'

Cleombrotus moves swiftly and confidently, almost gliding over the surface delivering a ferocious thrust of his sword into the attacking Helots' neck. The impact was so hard the handle of his sword was nearly embedded in to the flesh of the neck, lifting the Helot off his feet and slamming him to the ground. A cloud of sand and dust from the street surface erupts with an almighty *thud,* leaving the body motionless, dead.

'Our job is done here, Leonidas. We need to return to the Agoge,' Cleombrotus says, as he wipes the sweat and Helot blood of his face.

A Helot, who had been hiding since the Spartan soldiers arrived, shot out from a narrow side street, attempting to make an escape. 'Coward,' a voice bellows, from a distance.

It was Tiro, stepping forward with his pike, a spear of sort approximately seven feet in length; he casually adjusts his position, pivoting on his feet while simultaneously adjusting his grip.

His stance widens, and his balance is stable as he poises to throw his pike. His form is perfect, releasing the pike through the air chasing the Helot that continues to run, making a *swoosh* sound as it releases his hand. Tiro has perfectly judged the distance, wind direction and where the Helot will be by the time the pike reaches him.

The sun glares off the tip of the pike as it soars through the air. The Helot does not stand a chance, as the pike slams through the mid-section of his back and out of his chest. The Helot, still standing, eventually falls forward with the pike sticking into the ground, briefly holding him in position before falling on to his side.

'Let's get back to the Agoge now,' Tiro says, to the rest of the Spartan team with authority, as he runs over to fetch his pike.

'I wouldn't want to be the one cleaning this mess up,' Cleombrotus says out loud, progressing on.

'Things seem different around here, brother. Tensions have risen between Sparta and the Helots recently, more than usual,'

Leonidas says, with a concerned look on his face.

'These Helots just need reminding every now and again that we do not tolerate this here, in Sparta. I am sure Father has the city under control,' Cleombrotus says, confidently.

They gather their weapons as they walk the direction back to the Agoge.

'Wait Spartan,' says a feminine voice.

Leonidas turns to see the young Spartan woman he had previously saved.

'Thank you, Spartan, or shall I call you, Leonidas?' she says, as if she knows him.

'Yes, that is my name.' Leonidas struggles to recognise the lady.

'I do not expect you to remember me under the circumstances, it has been a long time and I have matured a lot since our last meeting.'

'Forgive me, my Lady.'

'No need Spartan. It is me, Gorgo.'

Gorgo is the daughter of Cleomenes, the half-brother to Cleombrotus and Leonidas. Much time has passed since Leonidas last laid eyes on Gorgo, most of which was spent training in the Agoge.

Cleombrotus, Leonidas and Tiro make it back to the Agoge where they are praised for their slaughter of the Helot slaves.

Spartans were often encouraged to leave the Agoge in order to steal food and livestock, and even kill Helots if they are found wondering at night, as it is considered likely they are out to rob the Spartans of their food and belongings.

Darkness falls, the night is particularly cooler than normal, winter is only a full moon away. The three of them bathe in a bath partially exposed to the outside, where all three sits in silence and reflect on the day's events. Leonidas stares in to the water, mesmerised by the gentle ripples that move over the reflection of the moon. It was a large, bright super moon and the craters that riddled the surface and much of their detail could clearly be seen.

Leonidas was in a state of day dream, watching the blood of his first Helot kill run off the surface of his skin and disperse in to the water.

Suddenly, there is a loud *Slap*. Tiro punches his fist in to the water, breaking up the perfect reflection of the moon, followed with a loud grunt, startling Leonidas out of his day dream.

'Wake yourself up, boy. I've been talking to you!' shouts Tiro, irritably. Leonidas does not respond and stands up to leave.

Cleombrotus follows, 'What is the problem, brother?'

'What makes you think there is a problem?'

'You have been distant ever since you slaughtered that filthy Helot,' Cleombrotus said, with a disgusting look on his face.

Leonidas pauses for a second, looking up to the God's followed by a sigh of frustration. 'I am clearing my mind of emotions, I've never killed a Helot before or any man for that matter,' he says, turning to Cleombrotus and diverting his line of sight to the floor.

'Snap out of it, you weak minded shit, you'll bring shame to the house of Agiad with those words!' Cleombrotus says, throwing his cloak on the floor he was using to dry himself with.

'I was also caught off guard, I didn't recognise Gorgo,' Leonidas says, with a tone of disappointment in his voice.

'You always were the weak, what, wait!' - stopping midway through his sentence - 'The young girl you saved was Gorgo?'

'Yes, that was her, brother. I wouldn't have noticed if she hadn't said anything.' Leonidas was disappointed that he hadn't noticed her, regardless of the circumstances.

'Many moons have passed since joining the Agoge; she has changed too. No doubt, learning our Spartan ways,' Cleombrotus says, while fidgeting his way in to his bedding.

Leonidas lay on his bed covering himself with his cloak, rolling on to his side. Peeking through a thin gap between the wooden slats, that make up the walls to the sleeping quarters, he focuses on the few stars he manages to see shining brightly, as if they are communicating to him in code.

There is the sound of muttering voices and tired groans throughout the sleeping quarters. The shadow of the overseer can be seen passing through the gaps in the wooden slats. He bangs twice on the wall, forcing the wall to vibrate and disperse a cloud of dust. As it settled, Leonidas could taste the dust on his lips.

The Sleeping quarters instantly fall silent and the faint sounds of an owl tooting, along with the overseer's footsteps, are the only sounds present.

Leonidas struggles to remain awake; his eye lids start to feel heavy as he fades in to a state of sleep, occasionally forcing himself to wake and observe the stars.

As Leonidas drifts in and out of sleep, he catches a glimpse of the owl he previously heard tooting. The owl was brilliant white and of good size. With its wings at full spread, the owl was able to glide effortlessly across the bright moon and in to the darkness.

He can't fight his tiredness any longer, as his eye lids become heavier, he drifts off with a single name on his mind, '*Gorgo.*'

3

Dong, Dong, Dong. The dreaded sound that echo's over the Agoge each morning, somewhat of a wakeup call. Tiro is already up, ready to fill his belly for the day's activities.

'Come on, get up!' yells Tiro, as he gives the boy next to him a swift kick in the ribs.

'Why do I get the impression he constantly feels he needs to prove himself?' Cleombrotus says, turning to Leonidas who is almost ready.

'We all need to prove ourselves, brother. That's why we are here.'

Leonidas steps out of the dorm to join his comrades at breakfast. The Overseer stops him abruptly, causing Leonidas to believe he has done something wrong.

'You have a visitor, make it quick!' he demands, as he turns and shoves Leonidas in the direction of the main gate.

As Leonidas steps out of the Agoge he welcomes the beautiful sight of the countryside. The mist hovers just above the ground as the sun begins to rise over the horizon, laying low as winter fast approaches.

To his left, he notices a figure waiting for him. Leonidas was struggling to identify who it was due to poor visibility and the intense morning sun silhouetting the figure, causing him to squint.

The figure moves closer towards Leonidas, he notices the long brown hair partially covering the individual's face, obstructed further with a silk white item over the head.

They stand just a few feet apart, as the individual looks up towards Leonidas, he feels a sense of warmth and his heart starts beating with a fluttering sensation.

'Gorgo, is that you?' he says, with a surprised but confused look upon his face.

'Why are you here?' he asks, without much care; he is just pleased to see her.

'I had to come and say thank you for what you did, I would be with the Gods now if it wasn't for you,' she said, with gratitude.

'In all honesty, I had no idea it was you. It all happened so fast,' replies Leonidas, as Gorgo lets out a small giggle.

'It has been a while Leonidas; I did not expect you to recognise me, I barely recognised you! You have been at the Agoge for some time now,' she says, anticipating a response.

Leonidas reflects briefly, 'Yes, I have, unfortunately it doesn't get any easier' – he looks behind, anticipating to be called back by the Overseer - 'No doubt much of your time is spent learning the ways of our Spartan women?'

'Yes, this is very true.'

'How is my Father?' a somewhat concerned Leonidas asks. 'I see frequent Helot revolts, which you are fully aware of?'

'Yes, although the size of the revolts never amounts to much, they are very disruptive and do not go unnoticed, especially by the Ephors.'

'I have previously heard and wondered myself whether or not my Father can manage for much longer. Our country is changing, and Athens political powers are overwhelming,' Leonidas says, in a concerned manner.

Gorgo replies with a stern voice, 'Sparta still stands, and we do not hide behind walls, we are more than heard, we are respected' - however, Gorgo still shares similar concerns - 'I overheard my Father talking to Brelos about the King and his level of competence; I certainly feel something isn't right.'

'Ah yes, Cleomenes, my Brother. Still has his opinions, I see,' Leonidas says, with frustration. 'We've never seen eye to eye, nor do I intend to.' Leonidas has never felt close to his brother, nor been given the chance to.

'I must go Leonidas; I only came to thank you; it has been good to see you.'

'Leonidas!' the Overseer shouts from a distance, interrupting his response to Gorgo.

Before he can manage to say anything, Gorgo leans in and kisses him gently on his lips.

Still lost for words, he places his hands on her shoulders applying a gentle, affectionate squeeze. Gorgo does not expect a reply and feels the words he is at a loss to say, are felt through his hands.

'I hope our paths cross again soon,' Leonidas thought to himself, as he watches Gorgo walk out of sight.

'Come on Leonidas,' the Overseer bellows, from a distance.

He runs back as fast as he can, he has missed the opportunity to feed himself and must go straight in to training.

'Make me call you twice again, I dare you,' the Overseer says through gritted teeth, holding Leonidas's arm to prevent him from running by.

'Your kind do not get the special treatment you think you deserve,' the Overseer says, knowing the lineage of Leonidas.

He joins back in with the training taking place out in the yard.

'Where have you been, brother?' an anxious Cleombrotus asks.

'Nothing that concerns you,' replies Leonidas, as he moves on to avoid any further confrontation.

Gorgo returns home, it is a busy household in the morning. Servants are sweeping off the last remains of leaves that still mingle around the edge of the yard. The servants hear Gorgo approaching and glance at her through their peripheral vision, realising she has made a trip that is out of routine. Their glances are not enough to make Gorgo notice and they remain sweeping, as if she went unnoticed.

'I called for you, Gorgo,' an irritated voice says, as she attempts to slip through the yard unnoticed.

'Sorry, Father, I had to pass on a message.' Cleomenes steps out from a doorway, towards her.

'Who needs a message delivered at this time of the morning?'

'Do not bother yourself with such menial information, Father. You have far more important things to consider, such as these

Helot slaves that keep planning their revolts within our city,' Gorgo suggests, hoping this ends his suspicions.

It is no secret Cleomenes and Leonidas are not the closest of allies, let alone brothers.

'Quite right, that's a valid observation,' he said, rolling his eyes at the thought of the revolts.

The opinion of Spartan women carried much respect within their culture and was not often questioned with doubt.

'An observation I saw with my own eyes, Father.' She turns and walks away, prompting the end of the conversation.

Another night is upon the Agoge, another tough day has passed, most are sleeping apart from the few whispers escaping the Overseers ears.

Cleombrotus is already in a deep state of sleep, bellowing out a snore, prompting Leonidas to nudge him to stop. Leonidas lays down, once again looking through the gap between the wooden slats, starring into the darkness.

The air is crisp, and the sky is clear. The breath of sleeping recruits can be seen drifting out above their cloaks.

The moon is bright enough to highlight larger objects, such as trees and roof tops with a tint of blue, enough light for Leonidas to once again notice the owl.

Leonidas observed the owl for what seemed a long time, watching it slowly tilt and turn its head. Suddenly, it swooped from the tree. This made Leonidas sit up on to his elbow, having never seen an owl hunt before.

The owl glided through the night without a single sound. Under its sharp talons was an area of dry long grass. Within a second, it landed into the grass with a *Crunch*. There was a moment of pause before the owl took flight again, with what seemed like a small rodent within its grasp.

'A perfect hunter,' thought Leonidas, as if he was learning something from watching the owl's perfect form.

Leonidas continued to observe the owl fly silently, close from where he was watching on the other side of the wall the owl found a post to rest on, picking at its meal.

Leonidas could not resist the urge to get a closer look; he clambered over the other recruits before managing to silently make way through the creaky door. He checked that no one was watching before making his way towards the owl. His punishment would be very severe should he be caught.

Eventually, Leonidas found himself just a couple of feet away from the owl, expecting the owl to fly away it remained on the post, calm and fearless.

'Beautiful,' Leonidas thought to himself, as he carefully observes the bird without startling it. The owl stood proud, grasping its kill tightly between its talons.

The first thing that struck Leonidas was the eyes, almost as if starring in to a clear night sky, with detail and clarity like nothing he has seen before. Somewhat hypnotic, Leonidas instantly felt this animal was here as a symbol when looking into its eyes, silently speaking to him, sent from the Gods.

The owl, still calm and unthreatened remained on the post, occasionally keeping itself occupied with the meal it caught shortly before. Leonidas took advantage of this and took a to step closer to walk around the animal.

From the front, its feathers were brilliant white and smooth looking; its beak was sharp and perfectly evolved for its craft.

As Leonidas gently moved around to the back of the owl, he observes its detail further. He notices its sand-coloured feathers with dark brown and black specks with occasional glimpses of white, whenever a gentle breeze blew, lifting the feathers slightly to reveal the white under layers.

Leonidas was fascinated; he had never observed such beauty. Suddenly, the owl opened its wings, blowing a gentle breeze over Leonidas's face. In a single beat of its wings, it had left silently, into the night.

Leonidas waited a moment before returning in the hope to catch another quick glimpse, to no prevail. As he lay back down to sleep, he could clearly hear the long call of the owl, a harsh sounding shriek. *'Tuto, a suitable name,'* thought Leonidas, still convinced it was a sign from the Gods.

Leonidas would sleep pondering his purpose beyond the walls of the Agoge.

4

Another year has passed, the winter harder than usual. The storms came early this year, covering Sparta and the surrounding hills and mountains with a dense layer of white snow.

The surrounding mountain range glistened in the low winter sun as it sparkled and reflected at the peaks. Mount Taygetus stood proud and was the largest mountain within the range, often used for defense and training purposes.

Leonidas is stood observing Mount Taygetus, focusing on the clouds of snow that dance around the mountain peak.

The sun was too low to feel the benefit of its warmth, the sky was clear and the air bitterly cold. Yet the snow is still gently falling, catching the attention of Leonidas as his vision focuses on a snowflake. The snowflake lands on to his hands that he has resting on top of a wooden post.

He observes the snowflake as it gently melts on to his skin and starts to run down his hand, Leonidas licks the melting snowflake off the top of his hands and closes his eyes, as if grateful for the cool sensation of water on his lips.

This reminds Leonidas of his childhood before the Agoge. For a moment he reminisces, spending his time along the Eurotus River, sipping the cool water that ran off the mountain ice melt to help quench his thirst.

Suddenly, there's an almighty *Crack*. The sound comes from the tip of a whip connecting and slicing through the flesh of Leonidas's back. He doesn't make a sound, nor does he for the next nineteen lashes. Heavy scarring on his back is visible from previous lashings, the healed wounds looking thick and tough from the countless repetitions of the overseer's whip. This is not a punishment, but a test of endurance; even the toughest of

Spartans have their limits. Leonidas starts to fade; he shakes his head to regain his vision. Leonidas passes the test.

Now in their late twenty's, Leonidas, Cleombrotus and Tiro were part of the same Syssitia, a social group for common meals, including thirteen other men of various ages. Leonidas and Cleombrotus often discussed the strange traditions within the Syssitia; however, this now made them eligible for military service.

'To think we've spent most of our lives in here Leonidas, training for war, learning to read and write,' Cleombrotus states, looking over to Leonidas who walks by his side.

'Yes, not forgetting the dozens of slaves we've butchered each autumn.'

'Ah yes, the Krypteia. I remember your first Helot kill,' Cleombrotus says, with a smirk.

'And I remember yours brother, he nearly sent you to visit the Gods.'

'Don't be stupid, Leonidas! The handle to my blade was nearly in his neck.'

'I often questioned the length of our swords, they never use to feel long enough,' laughs Cleombrotus.

'They are long enough to reach their hearts.'

'Correct, maybe I should stand closer,' Cleombrotus responds.

They pause, glance over at each other and burst into laughter, knowing full well there is nothing wrong with their ability to fight.

'Citizenship awaits Leonidas!' Cleombrotus states proudly.

'Thirty years of age,' Leonidas confirms.

'Not long Leonidas, not long.' They approach the barracks to join the rest of their unit.

They are greeted by Tiro; the three of them have become quite the trio, developing a fearsome reputation and outstanding abilities. 'Have you heard?' Tiro says, eager to tell.

'Heard what?'

'Agis was killed.'

Agis was a fellow Spartan who had trained alongside the trio throughout their time in the Agoge.

'He's dead, how is this?' Cleombrotus asks, in a surprised manner.

'The useless shit was killed by a fox, a fucking fox!' Tiro says, with an angry tone.

Agis had gone out looking for food and things to steal, something that was not out of the ordinary and a common way of life, for a Spartan. Only Agis had been caught, trying to steal while hiding the fox under his cloak. The fox had used its jaws and teeth on Agis's abdomen to try and escape. Instead of giving himself up as a guilty Spartan, he continued to hold the fox until his guts opened up. Agis would rather die knowing the fox had not been discovered, rather than suffer the humiliation of a fox under his cloak.

'What an idiot! he has made it this far and still manages to get killed by a fox. We are better off without him!' Cleombrotus says firmly.

'I agree, what use is he by our side on a battlefield if he can't handle a fox?' Leonidas shakes his head in disbelief.

'Anyway, I'm hungry. Let's go eat,' demands Tiro, as his stomach grumbles out loud.

Leonidas, Cleombrotus and Tiro arrive at the Syssitia for their daily ritual, everyone is in attendance, including the King who arrives late. Nobody dares question his timing.

Today is the end of the month, all Spartans must contribute to the phidites, this consisted of barley, wine, cheese and figs. Each Spartan is given a krelos, an allotment cultivated by a Helot slave. If any of the Spartans turn up short on their monthly contribution, they are excluded from the Syssitia until they can meet the monthly demand.

The Helot cultivating the krelos would also receive a thrashing and sometimes death, their fate left to the Spartan that has gone hungry. Fortunately, Leonidas, Cleombrotus and Tiro successfully make their monthly contribution.

The winter is starting to fade by the day but the evenings still provide a chill that rolls over the nearby mountains; Tiro has recently left the Syssitia and appreciates the fresh mountain air as he walks off a heavy meal, that sits awkwardly in his stomach.

Suddenly, Tiro is pounced on by a Helot that cowers at his feet; Tiro draws his weapon, but hesitates to strike the man who isn't showing an immediate threat.

The man was dirty, he looked hungry and cold. *'A typical Helot,'* Tiro thought to himself.

'Forgive me, please forgive me, I have been looking for the right opportunity for some time, Tiro,' the Helot says, desperately.

'What did you say?' Tiro asks, not sure he heard the man correctly.

The man fails to respond and looks to the floor.

'What did you say?' repeats Tiro. 'Answer to me or my blade, you shit!'

'I said please, forgive me. I have been looking for the opportunity to speak to you for some time, despite it possibly costing me my life,' the Helot man says, visibly shaking.

'You said my name, how do you know my name?' Tiro said, with some confusion.

The Helot man starts to cry as he tries to control his emotions and muster up the courage to speak.

'Please, clam yourself. I promise to not hurt you,' he says convincingly with a sympathetic approach, trying to coax the information out of the man. Tiro is now curious to what this ordeal is about.

'Stand up like a man and answer my question.' Tiro is getting impatient waiting for a response.

'I will ask you one more time and for your sake you best answer me. How do you know my name?' repeats Tiro.

The Helot man picks himself up off of the floor, looking up to the moon that brightly shines over Tiro's shoulder, 'Because I named you, my son,' answered the Helot man.

A huge wave of emotion passed through Tiro, almost like a heat wave coursing through his body. His heart rate increases to the point where he can feel it beating within his chest, his hearing fades, getting lost within his own thoughts.

'You are a lying piece of shit!' he shouts, cracking the handle of his blade on the side of the man's head, sending him back to the ground, unconscious.

The Helot comes around sometime later, struggling to sit up as he reaches up to the wound on his head. He focuses his blurry vision on to Tiro who is sitting on a boulder a few feet away.

'You didn't kill me, why?' the Helot man asked.

After striking the Helot man, a thousand questions entered his mind. Tiro took the time to compose himself and rested on the boulder, waiting for the Helot to wake.

They both sit in silence for several minutes in a state of shock, the Helot wondering if he should speak, and Tiro trying to comprehend the situation.

'Speak; give me cause for not cutting off your head.'

'My name is Orien. My wife Aglea and I originate from the city of Messene, where you were born.'

'This Aglea, you suggest she is my mother. Where is she?' Tiro asks curiously.

Orien briefly looked to the floor with an expression of sadness on his face. 'She died, from fever. I promised, I would fulfill her final wish to find her son and tell him the truth, she never got over the guilt.'

'Why should I believe you?' Tiro asks with a frown.

'Blindsiding a Spartan and telling him I am his Father is a quick way to have my head removed. A promise is a promise, regardless of its consequences.'

Tiro still looked confused and he was struggling to process what he has hearing. He was raised as a Spartan by an Ephor; his family was wealthy with a lot of influence. However, it wasn't unheard of for an adopted child to become a Spartan, providing they contributed enough to Sparta. *'Why did Father not tell me the truth from the very start?'* Tiro asks himself. Something just didn't seem right; he could feel it in his gut.

Orien moves closer to Tiro to comfort him, Tiro's upbringing would not allow for such weakness.

'Your parents are unable to have children; the God's would not permit it. I suffered a life changing injury falling from my horse and I could not provide for Aglea and you, our newborn son.' Orien looks on with an expression of guilt. 'You deserved better than what we had to offer. Your parents passed through the city, they noticed our struggle and offered to raise you as their own,' - he lets out a faint whimper - 'we were to receive payment, it never came, and I vowed to Aglea that one day I will find you.'

Tiro abruptly stands, kicking away a stone in frustration. he felt angry, betrayed.

'How did you find me?'

'I knew you would be raised as a Spartan, so it made sense I would find you here, but shocked to find they had not changed your name. It made my journey to find you much easier.'

Tiro was feeling emotions he wasn't quite sure how to deal with. This is one thing his training could not help him with and for the first time he felt powerless. Everything Tiro believed to be true has been a lie, his upbringing, ancestors and what he thought were his parents, all a lie.

Tiro was still pacing back and forth, he put his hands behind his head and took a deep breath, looking above the horizon, searching for answers he couldn't find.

'I must confront my Father, I need answers!' Tiro says through gritted teeth, still finding it difficult to comprehend the situation.

Without a word, Tiro walks off before pausing to turn and look at Orien. He hesitates and proceeds to walk on. Orien opens his mouth to say goodbye, he stumbles on his words and only manages to let out a sigh of frustration. He watches Tiro walk out of sight, wondering if their paths will ever cross again. If they didn't, he has at least fulfilled his promise to Aglea. Even if Tiro didn't believe him, the seed has been sown.

Orien picks himself up, happy that Tiro did not instinctively remove his head from his shoulders and hopes Tiro finds the answers he is looking for. He scratches the dry blood from his head wound with a smirk, *'He's strong,'* chuckling to himself before heading home.

Orien hears an unusual sound behind him, he stops to look but does not see anything. It is not unusual at this time of the evening to hear animals, so he ignores the noise and continues walking.

Suddenly, there is a sharp pain in between his shoulder blades, then a strike over his neck, knocking him to the ground.

His face hits the floor, splitting his lips and knocking out one of his front teeth. As he rolls over, he can see a figure standing over him but his vision is too blurry to make out any features.

Thick, dark blood oozes from his mouth and down his cheek; he hears a laugh followed by further pains in his abdomen. Orien remains on his back and looks down towards his feet, briefly holding his hands up to indicate to the person to stop. He observes the blade thrust in to his belly four more times, the blood pours and squirts from his wounds as he coughs up blood.

Orien starts to slip in and out of consciousness; the pain begins to fade, as does his vision.

The killer kneels over him and whispers in his ear, 'I knew someday you would come back and pay your son a visit. I've been watching you closely. Unfortunately, for you, your time is up.'

Orien must use the remaining strength in his entire body to turn his head to one side; his breathing becomes shallow and gradually slows down with each breath. He begins to see a vague image of Aglea leaning over him, stroking his face while encouraging him to come to her. The pain eases and the image of Aglea begins to fade, he knew his mind was deceiving him. The pain begins to return and Orien mutters his final words, 'Aglea.'

His vision slips away, the tunnel of darkness fast approaching; he gets a final look at the killer but does not recognise who he is. It is Brelos.

Brelos remains calm, dusts himself off and wipes the blood off his blade on Orien's tunic. Without a thought, Brelos walks away and leaves the body for the wolves.

A day has passed, and the weather has been hotter than usual. Tiro, Cleombrotus and Leonidas are all walking back the familiar route from the Syssitia, even more familiar to Tiro who met his Father here, just twenty a day earlier.

'Fuck, what is that stench?' Cleombrotus shouts, as they approach what looks like a pile of pig innards.

'Whatever it was, it made a good meal for the wolves,' said Tiro, not realising what he was looking at.

Leonidas followed the blood that has soaked into the sand and the drag marks left by the wolves' paws. Leonidas curiously followed them behind several large boulders. 'I found who those innards belong to. This poor bastard, or what's left of him,' Leonidas says, while pointing to indicate what he has found.

Cleombrotus walked over to Leonidas, 'Shit, poor bastard, looking at that tunic it was only a Helot.'

'Probably weak and lost at the time, wolves will take advantage of that,' Leonidas said, with a smirk.

Tiro approaches Cleombrotus and Leonidas from behind, his senses are heightened, and he feels a tight knot in this stomach.

Tiro's instincts are telling him what he doesn't want to confirm, as he looks over the shoulder of Leonidas, he instantly recognises the tunic as Orien's.

Tiro holds back any natural reaction so neither brother notices.

The corpse is face down, although a large percentage of it is missing. Tiro is still able to notice what looks like a typical stab wounds, he was familiar with this type of wound and he is surprised Cleombrotus and Leonidas did not spot it. Even if they did, Orien means nothing to them, he is just another Helot.

'Ah well, one less Helot for us to worry about,' says Leonidas. 'Let's get out of here I'm tired of the stench, even the wolves didn't want to finish him off,' Cleombrotus says, with a bellowing laugh, finding himself amusing.

'Who and why would someone murder him? So close to where we were talking, Orien has walked less than thirty feet before his death. We must have been watched,' Tiro thought to himself, with concern.

In Tiro's opinion this meant one thing, Orien was targeted for a specific reason and Tiro wants to know why, no matter the consequences. This indicates truth in what Orien said.

As Tiro turns to leave and catch up with the others, a bright glimmer of light shines across his eye, causing an array of colours to appear in his vision. On observation, he notices a small pendant partially buried in the sand.

Tiro pulls it from the sands while looking around to make sure nobody was watching. He checked to make sure the others were still walking. The pendant was of no value, but pretty, despite it being splattered in blood.

Tiro wipes his thumb over the pendant to rid the blood, exposing an image of a lion's head, on the reverse of the lion was a name engraved that read, 'Aglea.'

Tiro could not believe he had what he assumed was a gift from his Father to his mother, he knew he would never have the opportunity to meet his mother in this lifetime, but now he felt he had a part of her with him. Tiro places the pendant over his head and positions the lion on his chest, facing out. This gave Tiro a new sense of strength and belonging, he would see this through, no matter the consequences.

5

Several decades earlier, Brelos was a soldier marching in the ranks of the Persian army, the largest most feared army of all lands. Brelos sustained a serious injury during a battle on the Indian border where an arrow penetrated the base of his back, lodging the arrowhead firmly into his pelvis.

The arrowhead was never removed in its entirety and once healed left Brelos with a slight limp. Unfortunately, this left Brelos ineffective as a soldier and he was exiled from the military. This left a bitter taste in his mouth, Brelos knew nothing else but soldiering and had no other skills to fall back on.

However, Brelos was intelligent and a survivor who had a remarkable ability to turn his misfortunes around, but Brelos could not shake off his injury. He struggled to stay on his feet for long without his back having spasms and shooting pains down his legs.

Brelos made a decision to make a long journey to Athens with the intention to slip in to an established society, perhaps he could use his military knowledge to influence his way in to a position of authority or work closely with someone influential.

Brelos has the confidence and intelligence to do so and would happily advise the Athenians of Persian tactics since he was abandoned by the very thing, he was loyal to the most. This would be his leverage.

The journey took Brelos three months, a month longer than expected due to his injury. Some days were worse than others, but Brelos conserved his energy by stealing horses to ride and eating chickens and plant life he could scavenge under the protection of night. Despite his initiative, the journey took its toll on Brelos. Upon reaching the borders of Athens, he was in bad shape, filthy and weak, a far cry from his military days.

The sun had set and the breeze from the ocean was cooling the humid streets of Athens. Brelos made his way over to a makeshift shelter, some old market stands left over from previous markets that are no longer held.

Brelos was dehydrated and exhausted from the journey, it didn't take him long to collapse and fall into a deep sleep.

Sometime later, Brelos is woken by the sensation of a gentle rocking motion from side to side. The sun was rising, and he could feel the warmth radiate over his face, causing him to squint when a beam of sunlight penetrates his eye lashes, as he tries to focus on where he is.

He has been placed on a board and is being carried by several men; he is too weak to worry let alone put up a fight and drops his head down with a *thump*, falling back into a deep sleep.

Over the next few days, he slept and was being nursed to a standard of good health. Brelos woke and managed to sit himself up, 'where am I?' Brelos says to the domestic servant, helping him stand.

'Athens,' the young lady responds, with a confused look on her face. 'You're clearly not from around here, are you?'

Before he could respond he is interrupted by a man, Brelos assumes he is another household servant.

'Is he ready?' the man asks.

'Yes, but he needs a few moments to gather himself,' sheepishly directing her eyes towards the floor as if aware of Brelos's fate.

'Where am I going?' Brelos asks, anxiously.

The man backhands Brelos across the face, *Slap!* 'Shut your mouth, slave!' The man responds, sounding like an overseer.

Brelos paused to think about how to react, he kept his mouth shut knowing this is not the right time to announce he is an exiled Persian soldier; he would probably be accused of spying and killed on the spot.

Brelos was placed in fetters and loaded on to a wagon with several other men. 'Do any of you know where we are going?'

Brelos asks the other slaves on board. Nobody responds as they fear the consequences of talking.

'I am not a slave!' Brelos shouts, without receiving any attention. One of the slaves on board looks up at Brelos catching his gaze.

'If you want to live, shut your mouth. They are taking us to work at the quarries and mines, near Messene.' The slave whispers through gritted teeth, urging Brelos to be quiet.

Twelve months pass, fortunately for Brelos his limp was noticed early on and he was tasked with the occasional cutting of smaller stones and fetching water. This was something he could do with minimal effort while another slave removed the masonry on his behalf.

Despite an easier time than the other slaves, Brelos would spend his evenings in pain, as his muscles in his back would seize and spasm from the time spent on his feet.

Brelos would often think about how he could escape slavery, but he had nowhere and nobody to go to. For now, he planned to see it out until an opportunity presented itself.

That opportunity came sooner rather than later, part of the quarry had slipped away from the mountain side sealing a large section of the mine. There was an almighty *Bang* and a huge cloud of dust kicked up into the air, concealing everyone within the vicinity.

There was a lot of commotion and panic and badly broken arms and legs could be seen protruding from under the rocks, some still visibly twitching. Some of the rocks were so large there were no signs of anybody underneath them; accept a small stream of blood that had managed to find a way out through cracks in the ground. This was an opportunity Brelos could not afford to miss, before the dust even began to descend Brelos had breached the top of the quarry, he had escaped.

Nobody had seen Brelos escape, as far as he was concerned, he would be missing and assumed dead underneath the rubble. Brelos would not be missed. Slaves were easily replaced, and no effort would be made to find any survivors.

Several days pass and Brelos has done what he does best, survive. Brelos has put substantial distance between himself and the quarries, he feels relieved as he is sure a search would not be wasted on his behalf. Brelos decides to keep moving and follows a trail in to Messene. A small community with no major significance that would attract any unwanted attention.

As he approaches, he notices a fortified wall surrounding the community, built during previous conflict, but still used. Night is falling and Brelos decides to sleep under the cover of an olive tree outside of the walls, to allow him time to decide how not to draw any attention, unsure of how a small community would act with an outsider.

Now in complete darkness, Brelos lays on his back looking up to the night sky. The air is warm, and the sky is clear from any cloud coverage, exposing billions of stars and a moon so bright it almost casts shadows of objects on the ground. Brelos gazed endlessly into the night, it suddenly dawned on him that he was completely alone and had nothing to his name. *'I could pass in my sleep and when found, nobody would be none the wiser, completely insignificant,'* Brelos thought to himself.

Brelos began to drift in and out of sleep, holding a rock in one hand in case of unwanted visitors, human or animal approached. Above the gentle noise of crickets chirping, he hears the nearby sound of running water. He sits up and follows the sound to a spring. He falls to his knees, cups his hands to scoop the water and throws it over his face while swallowing large gulps to quench his first.

After having a wash, Brelos lay's down by the spring but is unable to sleep with a heavy belly full of water, Brelos consumed enough to hear the *swashing* sound inside of him whenever he decided to move.

As Brelos attempts to sleep, his eyes scroll around the vicinity and he notices a couple of old buckets on the bank of the spring, partially submerged in the water. This urges Brelos to move out of sight and choses to rest above the spring. He assumes the spring is still used and did not want to be in sight of any users that may make an early morning stroll to fetch water.

Day breaks, Brelos could hear the sound of walking, soles scuffing along the ground towards his location. Looking over the edge of the spring, he notices some of the locals have come to collect water.

Brelos judges quickly, and decides these people are not a threat to him as he stands and walks down the rocky path towards them.

There are four locals present, all stop to observe Brelos. Despite already washing in the spring, it was obvious he had suffered; his eyes instantly gave that away and his clothes and footwear were not in the best of condition.

One of the locals pulled the bucket he noticed the previous night out of the spring, and then washed it out before handing it to Brelos. He indicated to Brelos to collect some water and follow on.

They didn't feel the need to speak and this put Brelos at ease, instantly developing a trust. *'If they didn't want me here, they would have drawn attention to themselves by now,'* Brelos thought to himself, not sure whether he is just trying to convince himself. He keeps the rock in his hand for the time being and follows the locals through the community walls.

As Brelos enters the community, he keeps his wits about him observing as much as he can. It was clear the community was poor, but well organised, and old relics of previous times were left exposed, almost intentionally as a reminder of their past.

'My name is Adonis, what's yours?' one of the locals that walked in with him asks.

'Brelos,' he says, while looking over his shoulder.

'Brelos, Ok, I notice you are hesitant and a little anxious. I'm not making any assumptions, but you are a free man here and welcome,' Adonis says, with affection.

Brelos lets out a sigh of relief and begins to relax. 'May I have some new clothes, if you have any spare?' Brelos asks reluctantly.

'Yes, I have something for you, please, follow me,' said Adonis, walking with his arm out straight indicating the direction for Brelos to walk. 'You can stay here for now, for as long as you wish. My wife and son recently passed from a fever, so I have the room,' said with sad eyes and half a smile, as if briefly seeing his family within his thoughts.

'Why are you helping me?'

'Look around you Brelos, we have nothing of worth here except land and a spring, sometimes the spring is used as a stopping point for travelers. We are mainly farmers living in an old fortified community; we are no threat to anyone.'

Brelos reaches out to shake Adonis's hand. 'Thank you, brother.'

Several weeks have passed, Brelos is loyal to helping Adonis farm the land and handle livestock, but he still knows this is not his destiny. However, he uses the stay to his advantage.

Brelos now appears well fed bringing him back to good health, he has regained his stocky physique and despite still having a limp, he has few occasions where he must rest his injury.

'The rumour is we have a Spartan Ephor on his way here, with his wife. They will be stopping for water at our spring on their way back from Athens,' Adonis says excitably, never seeing anyone of that caliber here before.

'Is that so?' replies Brelos.

'Yes, a farmer from this community was returning from selling cattle at the market, he was asked by the Ephor if he knew of a place to stop on route for water, an unexpected stop due to his horse being unwell.'

The next morning the Spartan Ephor approaches, instructing his Helot servant to fetch some water while he attends his lame horse.

The leader of the community comes out to welcome the Ephor and his wife. 'Welcome to Messene, Sir. How can I assist?' he says nervously.

'My name is Cicero, Ephor of Sparta. This is my wife Rhea, she has an appetite,' Cicero hints to the leader.

'Certainly, Sir,' he replies, ordering fresh fruit to be fetched. A young girl approaches carrying a small basket of fruit in one hand and a child, no older than a week or two, in the other. The young girl hands the basket of fruit to Rhea.

'What a beautiful looking child,' Rhea compliments to the young lady.

'Thank you, his name is Tiro,' replied the lady, shying away from Rhea, looking down at the floor.

Rhea noticed how tired and out of depth the young girl looked with her baby. *'Having a baby so young, must be hard for her especially with such limited wealth,'* Rhea thought to herself.

Although Rhea does not show it, she is extremely envious of the young lady; Cicero and Rhea are unable to conceive. They had everything, wealth, status, influence, but none of that could buy them the happiness that a baby would bring.

Cicero needed to rest his horse; they stayed the night in Messene, with the intention to move on at day break.

Rhea was not happy to stay; Cicero had slept in worse places especially during his time in the Agoge.

That evening, Brelos could not sleep and decided to go for a walk around the community. The streets were dark, with the occasional flicker of candlelight in a few window openings.

Suddenly, Brelos could hear bickering coming from the house Cicero and Rhea were staying in. He approached the house and noticed Cicero's servant asleep on the floor just within the doorway, unfazed by the bickering. Brelos moved to one side, hiding himself within a shadow, as Cicero left the house. Cicero looked suspicious, looking around to make sure nobody was watching; he carried a leather pouch that Brelos assumed had gold inside, he could hear coinage when Cicero stepped out of the house.

Brelos followed Cicero; at times he looked lost, before he approached another house, he made sure he wasn't being watched. Cicero entered the house prompting Brelos to sneak up to the doorway to observe Cicero. *'What is he up to?'* Brelos questioned himself, baffled by Cicero's behaviour. Brelos took a big breath, hoping he would not be seen before looking around the door. He could see Cicero in a small room, through another doorway.

Brelos noticed the young girl who took out the fruit, hours earlier; she was sleeping next to the Father. He observed Cicero place the pouch of gold on the floor and takes the young girl's baby. Brelos could not believe his eyes. *'Fuck the God's!'* Brelos thought. It took Brelos a matter of seconds to figure out how he could use this to his advantage, but a risky position to place himself in to.

The baby did not wake, and Cicero cautiously starts to leave the house. Brelos runs behind a partially fallen stone column, kneeling low enough not to be noticed.

Cicero takes the baby back to Rhea, 'Now what?!' Making it obvious this had not been thought through properly.

'Keep your voice down, we will raise him through the Spartan regime as one of our own. You know we can provide a better life for this boy, his very own mother is a child,' Rhea says, convincing Cicero in the process.

Rhea covers the baby; Cicero turns to the door to wake his servant and see's Brelos standing in the doorway over him. The servant stirs and abruptly wakes when noticing Brelos over him, Brelos delivered a single kick to the servant's jaw, putting him straight back to sleep.

'Well, well, well. Not only have I caught a Spartan stealing, I've caught an Ephor and his wife stealing, a baby!' Brelos states, with a smug look on his face. 'This would bring much dishonour should this get back to Sparta.' Hinting at wanting something in return.

'Do you know who I am?!' Cicero says in a stern, threatening manner.

'I couldn't give a fuck! What I do know is the dishonour and shame being caught stealing brings to a Spartan.'

The look on Cicero's face proved he was right, already showing shame, as he lets out a sigh.

'What do you want?' Cicero reluctantly asks Brelos.

Rhea steps forward, obstructing him. 'Don't offer this man a thing! It's his word against ours!'

Brelos stands firm, arrogantly folding his arms confidently looking in to Cicero's eyes, knowing he will get what he will ask for.

Cicero pulls Rhea to one side. 'Well then?' Cicero says, as if he has places to be.

'Your secret will always remain safe with me Ephor, on the basis you provide me with a monthly payment of gold,' Brelos demands, with certainty and a smile from ear to ear.

'How, when and where?' Cicero responds, wanting more details.

'Well, that's the catch, I want you to take me back with you and provide me with a reputable position. I have limitations with an old injury, but will happily serve someone with authority who can provide me with the quality of life I deserve.'

'Never!' shouts Rhea.

'Quiet Rhea! Ok, as it happens, I know of a position. However, I want something from you besides your guarantee of secrecy.'

'Ok,' replies Brelos, not quite believing his bluff has paid off.

'If I need you for any 'dirty work' I expect you to come, no questions asked,' Cicero demands.

Cicero and Brelos reach out to shake arms to signify a made deal. However, Rhea walks between the two breaking up the arm shake while carrying baby Tiro away, to signify her dislike.

The morning sun breaks over the Messene horizon, creating a beautiful orange outline on the distant hills. Orien and Aglea are woken by the singing of the early birds; the air is cool, as much of the community is still in shadow, waiting for the sun to rise above the walls.

Instantly, they notice Tiro has gone and is replaced with a large pouch that is tied shut. Aglea leaps out of bed, frantically searching for her son while tears immediately stream down her face. 'Where's our son, Orien?' Aglea asks, as she observes Orien opening the pouch.

'It's gold Aglea, lots of gold,' Orien says in disbelief. His face lights up with a yellow glow reflecting off the precious bullion. As Orien scoops a handful of coins out to show Aglea, he pulls out a note.

'We see the struggle to provide for your child, but we also see the love. Show your love and let us provide the life he deserves and one you will never be able to afford. Do not search for him.'

The note was selfishly written by Rhea in a way that makes her appear to be doing Tiro a favour. The reality, Rhea wants a child and Cicero wants that child to be a son. They would do anything to have one.

Orien and Aglea embraced each other in tears, knowing they would never see or be able to retrieve their son again. However, a small piece of Orien felt relieved, knowing that his son would be fed and provided for. He kept his feelings away from Aglea. She would never get over the loss of Tiro.

Back in Sparta, there were no questions who Tiro belonged to. Cicero and Rhea would tell the story of how she gave birth to Tiro while travelling, not realising she was with child. It was a blessing from the Gods.

Cicero was able to place Brelos in the King's service. Brelos would replace the King's previous servant who had recently died of natural causes.

This was exactly where Brelos wanted to be, being the King's servant was not like any other servant in Sparta. It was a privilege and Brelos would use his new position and the King's poor health, to his advantage. It wouldn't take long before winning the Kings trust.

6

Leonidas has been to visit his Father where he is concerned his ever-decreasing health is making the house of Agiad look weak and vulnerable. Raising further concerns about potential challenges with Athens and the Eurypontid dynasty.

Leonidas approaches the house where he is welcomed by Brelos; Leonidas can hear his Father violently coughing. Brelos acknowledges Leonidas's presence with a bow but says nothing.

The King appears to be unsettled, frustrated with his health. Leonidas observes him for a moment pacing around the room while muttering to himself. Leonidas shakes his head and begins to question his Father's sanity.

'Hello, Father!' the King turns around sharply, not realising Leonidas was there.

'Yes. Oh, hello Son. What brings you here?' the King replies. The King looks dreary, pale and his hair appears frizzy from the sweat. Leonidas notices a significant different in his health which appears to deteriorate on every visit.

'Father, you look terrible. I speak as a son with concerns, people are starting to realise how weak you have become. Medicines are not working; citizens are beginning to create rumours.

The King looks disgruntled but doesn't respond, he knows his words are true.

After a few moments the King replies, 'You sound like your mother,' he laughs, interrupted by further coughing. 'I refuse to step down, I am King and regardless of what anyone thinks, I am more than coping!' he says, in an irritated manner.

'The people of Sparta don't want you to cope Father, they want you to rule. You are their symbol of strength, if your weakness is realised by the Helot population this will undoubtedly start further riots. These are already a frequent problem.' The King waves his hands in frustration, indicating for Leonidas to leave. 'I don't want to hear it, Leonidas.'

'*Stubborn as ever,*' Leonidas thought to himself, as he walks away.

He passes his mother on the way out where she forces him to stop. 'Mother, he is in no shape to rule as King. The stubborn fool is making the house of Agiad appear weak. If the Helots hear about this; we will have riots on unprecedented levels,' Leonidas says, frustrated.

The Queen puts her hands-on Leonidas's chest to comfort him, as she is about to speak Leonidas interrupts. 'This needs to be addressed by the Ephors, my brothers' and I will not take the fall for this!' Leonidas turns away from his mother, extending his stride to walk away faster.

Brelos hears everything and he leaves the Queen to attend the King, and other business, with a smirk on his face.

Leonidas is seething and there is only one person he wants to see, someone who listens to him and has an ability to calm his temper instantly. He walks towards the stables where he knows she'll be attending to her horse; she spends much of her time there.

Leonidas approaches the stables. Before entering, he observes her through a crack in the door. He watches her for some time, the sun was casting a single beam of light through the window to her side whilst she stands alongside the white stallion, brushing it gently.

The horse was brilliant white, strong and muscular and gave the illusions to be glowing, as the beam of sunlight landed upon its back.

Leonidas walks through the door; the young lady was happy to see him. Leonidas observed her beauty some more, she had thick black hair that hung halfway down her back that was shiny enough to see your reflection in. Part of her hair was in a large singular plait, perfect, intertwined with gold thread. Her skin was porcelain smooth and tanned; her eyes were so dark they appeared black like large sapphires. Leonidas greets her with a kiss and places his hand over her heart, she is equally happy to see him. 'Your sheer beauty calms me instantly, my love,' he says, gazing in to her eyes.

'I don't feel beautiful, but you always did know what to say,' replies Gorgo, acting shy.

Leonidas and Gorgo have been in a discrete relationship for several months. They do not want Cleomenes to know, despite being perfectly matched in every way. Gorgo brings balance to Leonidas and she gives Leonidas the drive to see Sparta succeed, even more than usual. Hence, his frustrations with his Father.

'How is your Father?'

'He isn't improving, in fact he is progressively getting worse. He refuses to acknowledge his health and the impact it could potentially have...is having!' Leonidas says, correcting himself.

'Oh, what are his options?'

'Not many Gorgo, not many,' he replies, stroking the nose of the horse. 'A fine beast,' he says, patting the side of the horse's head.

'He sure is,' she agrees.

'I wasn't talking about the horse,' he says laughing.

'Very funny, I'll retract my previous statement about you always knowing what to say.' She pushes Leonidas out of the way, with a smile.

Leonidas embraces Gorgo and kisses her on the forehead and turns to leave, momentarily putting his palm under the horse's nose, as he passes him on his way out.

Leonidas needs to find Cleombrotus and discuss the position their Father is placing Sparta in.

Leonidas and Cleombrotus have struck up quite the relationship over the years and have become reliant on one another. A relationship that is often frowned upon in Spartan society. However, Leonidas has little trust in anyone other than

Gorgo, but there is a connection with Cleombrotus he cannot deny.

As far as Dorieus and Cleomenes are concerned, Leonidas was not so sure, and it was no secret the two elder brothers clashed. Dorieus and Cleomenes did not pay too much attention to Leonidas and Cleombrotus, they are somewhat insignificant in the pecking order and this was made obvious at every available opportunity.

Leonidas locates Cleombrotus, as they approach each other they pause for a moment. There is a rumbling sensation beneath their feet, they observe the dust and small stones dance around their ankles followed by a loud cracking noise. Lasting no more than a few seconds the tremor is gone before most even realise what it was. Cleombrotus observes the nearby hills, watching a few lose boulders roll down to the base of the hill.

'A reminder from the God's brother, they still watch us,' says Cleombrotus, shrugging it off with a smile.

'Wouldn't surprise me, the way Father is portraying himself,' Leonidas says angrily, concentrating on whether he can still feel the tremors.

'Yes, mother told me you had made a visit. I must have just missed you, when I had arrived.'

'He grows weaker by the day, too weak to rule but too strong to die. I can't help but wonder if he is fit to be King anymore, the alternative however, is not much better,' states Leonidas, grabbing his chin and pulling down on his beard in frustration.

'It's either Cleomenes or Dorieus? Not exactly spoilt for choice here, at least Dorieus is full blood.'

There was not much love from the two of them towards their elder brothers; Cleombrotus hated Dorieus more so due to his lack of respect he frequently showed to the Spartan regime. However, Cleomenes is an excellent tactician.

Suddenly, there was a sense of unease in the atmosphere. Nearby cattle became unsettled and the pigs in a nearby pen started to squeal aggressively. The ground began to tremble once more and at first seemed minimal; the tremor gradually began to grow in strength creating a sound like a clap of thunder. The ground shook violently sending people into a panic. Fences collapsed and livestock started to escape.

Cleombrotus places his hand on Leonidas's shoulder, before hearing an almighty *crack!*

They both observe a small crack, no wider than a finger, opening across the ground running between their legs. The dust and rubble on the ground appeared to be alive as it danced across their path, falling down the crack that began to get deeper. Then silence.

It took some time for the citizens to compose themselves and most of them had not experienced such an event, left confused and frightened.

The event only lasted a few moments. Unbeknown to Sparta, this was merely a tremor and a potential sign of something greater to come.

'Nothing to be concerned about brother, we need to focus on the bigger problem, our Father,' Leonidas requested, hoping to get approval from Cleombrotus.

'You mean the Ephors?' Cleombrotus asks, folding his arms.

'Yes, the Ephors.'

The two of them decide to speak with the Ephors before arriving at the Syssitia that evening. Leonidas and Cleombrotus enter the council later in the evening, the Ephor servants preparing food to take to the evenings Syssitia. Leonidas suddenly notices Brelos, leaving the premises from another exit. *'Brelos?'* Leonidas questions himself.

The five Ephors are sat around a table deep in conversation, discussing issues before having to leave. All were loyal to Sparta first and foremost, then the two Kings of Sparta, who were also classed as Ephors. However, it was not uncommon for the five Ephors to discuss politics without the Kings as the two Kings rarely cooperated with each other. The Ephors stopped talking when they noticed the brothers' approach, Cicero turns to greet them.

'Leonidas, Cleombrotus, I was expecting you. I hear you have concerns?' Cicero was a much-respected member of the Spartan regime; he was previously one of the elders within the Gerousia before being elected as an Ephor.

'Why was Brelos here?' Leonidas asks, suspiciously.

'Not your concern.' Cicero appears to quickly brush off the conversation. Little did they know Brelos was there to collect his bribe and reassure Cicero that Tiro's Father, has been dealt with and nobody else is any the wiser.

Cleombrotus diverts the conversation back to why they were there. 'We are concerned about our Father's health, he is making poor decisions and barely has the strength to get out of bed, let alone rule Sparta.'

'As Ephors, please discuss what is best for Sparta.'

'You want us to discuss the potential downfall of your own Father?' the Ephors glance at each other, giving the brothers a sense that they are clearly aware and already have plans in place.

'Our Father is a King first; he serves Sparta, as do we.' Cicero smiles and turns to sit back down at the table, almost disregarding the issue with his body language. Propping his elbow on to the table and placing his chin in his palm to hold his head up.

Cicero looks around the table at the other Ephors who say nothing, 'Thank you for addressing your concerns.' The conversation closed.

Leonidas and Cleombrotus start to walk backwards with a nod of respect, as Cleombrotus turns away Leonidas hesitates.

'Please, consider the consequences.' Sensing the Ephors were not taking their concerns seriously enough.

As Cicero turns to address Leonidas, he is interrupted by one of the other Ephors who stands and addresses Leonidas with aggression.

'Do not be mistaken, boy. You were merely allowed to enter this council based on your connection to the King. I wouldn't expect you to understand our political relationship with Athens right now; we are part way through a truce that was instigated by your 'weak' Father. How would Sparta look if we replaced the King, which is what you're suggesting, right? The only thing I will be considering is how many lashes you will receive if you are not gone by the time I blink!'

'Come brother,' pulling Leonidas's arm, encouraging him to turn away. They both leave the council with their tails between their legs.

'Shit! What are you trying to achieve Leonidas? I have enough scars thank you! Do you not feel you look battle hardened enough yet?'

The walk home seemed long and the two barely spoke a word. Leonidas was reflecting on his approach; he was made to look stupid and realised his political knowledge was minimal. Deals with Athens are on a need-to-know basis and he didn't need to know. Regardless, Leonidas knew politics enough to realise the Athenians could not be trusted. They would not hesitate to undermine this truce, if they haven't already.

'This is bullshit Cleombrotus; the Athenians probably have spies all over this region, what good is a truce? Seems to me Father wants an easy option, always avoiding the conflict. Before we know it, we will be eating out of Athenian palms!' Leonidas says, angrily airing his frustrations.

Cleombrotus continued to walk by his side in silence; he felt like he couldn't contribute to the matter any further. What was done, was done.

Both knew the King's health would continue to deteriorate and they would both have to keep hoping by the time this happens, it's not too late for Sparta.

The atmosphere could be cut with a knife as Leonidas and Cleombrotus feast at the Syssitia, weighed down by their concerns for their Father, more importantly, Sparta.

'Am I missing something?' Tiro says, with a mouthful of food.

'Yes, the food hanging off your chin,' says Alec, one of the fellow Spartans. Everyone around the table but Tiro, laughs. Leonidas and Cleombrotus manage to break into a smile trying not to give anything away. Alec quickly silenced when he didn't get the reaction, he was expecting from Tiro.

Alec was a very slim Spartan, almost too skinny, but very well defined and exceptionally fast with his blades. He was below average height and always carried two daggers, one on each hip approximately ten inches in length. Despite looking like he lacked strength due to his lack of muscle mass, he was known to take on opponents twice his size with excellent hand to hand combat abilities, mainly due to his blistering hand speed and beast like aggression.

Tiro shifted uncomfortably over to Leonidas, he had known him and Cleombrotus long enough to know something was on their minds. Tiro automatically assumed it would be something to do with the family. There are all sorts of pressure and expectations that come from being part of their lineage, everyone was aware of this. Leonidas and Cleombrotus have gained huge respect over the years, especially through their journey within the Agoge and how they have handled themselves. They've not taken advantage of their lineage, nor have they been given an easy time. If anything, they have had it harder than most.

'Leonidas, what is on your mind today, brother?' Tiro asks, giving Leonidas a friendly tap on the back for encouragement.

'Do not concern yourself with my problems my friend.' Sipping from his cup to avoid any further conversation.

Cleombrotus leans in to join in on the discussion, 'It isn't necessarily your problem, brother.'

Tiro looks at Cleombrotus who shrugs his shoulders, he then looks at Leonidas with widened eyes, attempting to prompt Leonidas to elaborate. Cleombrotus takes it upon himself to speak on behalf of Leonidas. 'We went to the council to address a family concern, with the Ephors.'

'You addressed the Ephors? Why would you need to do such a thing?' - Not expecting to hear what they had done - 'I am guessing you did not get the response you hoped for. I am more surprised you haven't been lashed; it's not your place to address the council! You must be mad!' Leonidas glances at Tiro with a blank expression.

'Well, let's just say that was a strong possibility at the time,' states Cleombrotus.

'Cicero brushed me aside, but I still stand by my concerns,' Leonidas replies, clenching his fists and banging it on the table surface.

Tiro felt awkward, he had always kept himself to himself and never spoke about his private life, but somehow felt responsible for what had happened that day. Although Spartans develop a bond of brotherhood, it is never deemed necessary to talk about one's family. Unfortunately for Leonidas and Cleombrotus, it was nearly impossible to hide, everyone knew.

'You spoke to Cicero?'

'Yes, asshole brushed me off,' looking at Tiro, oblivious to who his Father is.

'Oh, right.' The atmosphere felt thicker with awkwardness as Tiro rolled his eyes around the room.

'Cicero is my Father,' announces Tiro, waiting for their response.

Cleombrotus claps his hands twice with an awkward laugh, 'You are the son of an Ephor?' Well, I be damned; you learn something new every day.'

Leonidas was initially shocked; he wasn't expecting to hear such a thing but it makes no difference to Leonidas or any other Spartan. They have all been through the Agoge and are classed as equals. Nobody else seems to respond despite hearing what was just mentioned, they all share the same passion, serving Sparta.

'Yes, he is my Father,' he said, without going into the details of Orien, he didn't want to embarrass himself further.

'Let's go home brother, perhaps when you get home you can ask your Father why Brelos, my Father's servant, was there,' Leonidas says jokingly, but with some seriousness. Leonidas could sympathise with Tiro, having a parent who carries that level of authority can often become a burden.

'Why would my Father have any business with Brelos? I have questions I need answering, I need to speak with him as soon as possible,' Tiro thought to himself, thinking of all the questions he must ask.

The following day Tiro approaches his Father, feeling slightly apprehensive about how he would react. Tiro already knew his Father was keeping secrets from him, but why was there a need to cover it up for so many years. Tiro felt angry, the only reason he knows is because Orien tracked him down. There was clearly a plan to have him killed whether he had tracked Tiro down or not.

'Father, I need a moment of your time,' he says filling his lungs with as much air as possible. Cicero could see something was on Tiro's mind.

'Now is not the time,' replies Cicero, not even making the effort to look at Tiro in the eyes. Cicero starts to walk away to attend other matters, he is meeting with the council to discuss the Athenian truce further.

'Will there ever be a right time, Father?' Cicero stopped in his tracks as he sensed the sarcasm in which Tiro pronounced Father. He turns to face Tiro.

'You know, don't you? It was that bastard servant Brelos, wasn't it? I knew I couldn't trust him!' Tiro looked confused, he wasn't sure who Cicero was referring to until the conversation he had with Leonidas sprung to mind.

Tiro looked puzzled, 'Brelos?'

'He didn't tell you?' Now Cicero appeared to be the confused one, not knowing how Tiro knows.

'Why the hell would Brelos have anything to do with this? You are not making any sense Father!' The tension between the two was becoming increasingly uncomfortable; Trio had gone to find answers and was now presented with more questions. Cicero approached Tiro and started to ask a question, 'How do you....' Cicero suddenly stops as he notices the pendant around Tiro's neck. He appeared to recognise the pendant but was unable to immediately determine where from. A few seconds pass until Cicero remembers, he recalls seeing Aglea wearing it in her sleep the night he took Tiro.

'That's impossible,' Cicero mutters to himself.

Tiro notices Cicero's eyes fixed on to his pendant as he reaches up and grasps it in his hand.

'You must be wondering how I have this. You obviously recognise it?' Cicero appears angry, humiliated. 'I found this on my real Father's remains, shortly after you butchered him and left him for the wolves!' Tiro says, pointing into Cicero's chest.

'No, no, no that's not how it happened,' Cicero stutters, trying to find an explanation. 'It's more complicated than that, I had no choice.' Cicero starts to pace around trying to justify his actions, he places his hand on his forehead in a display of disbelief.

'I was going to tell you one day Tiro, when the time presented itself.' Tiro was not convinced in the slightest.

'There's always a choice, it's your job to make choices!' states Tiro, keeping his temper at bay.

'I did not kill your Father, Tiro.' Cicero's eyes briefly connect with Tiro's, before looking away.

'But you know who did?' the answer suddenly presented itself to Tiro, as if placed in front of him. 'Brelos, you got Brelos to do your dirty work. That's why he has been sneaking around and exiting through back doors.' Things started to become clearer for Tiro, but questions still remained unanswered.

There was a moment of silence; both were taking in what was unfolding before them. Cicero was caught off guard and was late attending the council.

'This will have to wait Tiro, I will explain all on my return.' Cicero storms off while cursing under his breath.

Tiro was left standing on his own; a breeze had picked up gently passing through, cooling off his face from the sweat that has accumulated on his forehead and over the bridge of his nose. He felt a mix of emotions and it would take some time to come to terms with what he now knows, but questions remained, and he would stop at nothing to get the answers he is after. Despite not knowing his birth parents, Tiro felt obliged to do good by them.

Tiro paced around feeling confused and torn between who he thought he was and who he actually was.

Tiro takes a moment to question his purpose and reminisces on all the pain and endurance he has suffered through his upbringing as a Spartan. It suddenly felt unnecessary, but he knows his duty is as a Spartan. He knows no other life.

7

Two days have passed; there is a sense of unease in the air around Sparta, the birds and livestock silent and inactive.

The breeze that has reached inland from the coast, blows the sand through the streets with energy in mesmerising fashion, before clashing with the walls and dropping to the floor, suddenly lifeless.

A tense atmosphere looms over the city. Despite this, citizens and slaves go about their business as usual.

The Ephors have been in conversation regarding the previous tremors, concerned the Helot's would revolt and try to take advantage of such misfortune. Not in Sparta.

A decision was reached to move hundreds of Spartan warriors out of the city the moment any new tremors were felt, this allowed a reserve of soldiers to be on standby, on the off chance they would be needed.

'Bastard Helot population,' curses the King, as he returns to the house, nobody but Brelos to return conversation.

'Is there a problem, my King?' asks Brelos, eager to encourage the King to share what has been discussed with the Ephors.

The King looked weak, Brelos was surprised the King made it out in his condition.

'They cause problems, even when they aren't intentionally causing problems. Ridiculous!' the King says, with ire.

'I was under the impressions things were settling, in that respect, my King?' asks Brelos.

'You and I both, You and I both. We are preparing for hundreds of our warriors to leave the city if these tremors are to continue, the tremors seem to rattle the Helot population.'

'I see,' responds Brelos, scratching the back of his neck. Evening falls, Brelos decides to write a message to Athens under candlelight, using a messenger pigeon he has contained in a small cage, self-made from sticks.

The message read; 'The God's have answered and tremble our land, soon to destroy I'm sure. Sparta will evacuate hundreds of soldiers, reserved for potential revolt. The King will die. Put Athenian army on standby. Sparta will be vulnerable. From Brelos, your loyal servant.'

Brelos grabbed the bird from the cage; the bird was frequently handled and remained calm. Brelos gave it some food and checked its wings before rolling up the message and tying it to the pigeon's foot. As Brelos approached the balcony, bird in hand, he felt the ground shudder. *'Was that my imagination?'* Brelos thought to himself, placing the bird back in the cage so he could observe properly.

Across the way, Gorgo is taking in the night air. She too felt the ground shudder, but it felt too small to consider anything more serious. *'Damn Gods,'* she thought.

Shortly after, Gorgo could hear marching in the distance, the sound of leather soles slapping the ground, echoing through the streets. Gradually, increasing in volume, the sound draws closer. The shudder was enough to put the mass of soldiers on standby, as voted by the Ephors. Gorgo observed the soldiers march towards the city border, a single file of red cloaks and shields.

The Spartans were drawing local attention, anyone that is observing would assume the soldiers were off to settle a conflict in a faraway land, not to sit in wait for a revolt that may or may not happen.

Citizens started to mutter and whisper to one another, trying to guess where the Spartans were heading. Most assumed they were heading towards Athens, it was no secret the relationship between both cities was tense, despite there being a truce.

Gorgo turns to head back into the house just as Leonidas returns. 'Where have you been?' she asks Leonidas. 'I was expecting to see you among the ranks that just passed; I was concerned I had not heard from you.'

'Apologies, Cleombrotus and I had things to settle at the Agoge, but we must join with the ranks leaving the city. Don't concern yourself my love,' Leonidas says convincingly, as he kisses Gorgo and leaves to join the ranks.

Gorgo catches a glimpse of Cleombrotus over Leonidas's shoulder. He was acting suspicious as though he didn't want to be seen.

Cleombrotus quickly acknowledged Gorgo with a respectful nod, before following Leonidas. Gorgo returned a nod and noticed what appeared to be blood on Cleombrotus's hands. Gorgo immediately thought this appeared strange, why would he not bathe at the Agoge before leaving covered in blood. However, it is not out of the ordinary to see a Spartan with blood on his hands and she thought no more of it, as she watched the Spartans march out of the city. The sound of marching slowly fading into the distance, suddenly, they are no longer heard.

The evening draws in, the air is cool and crisp and the sky is clear. The moon is appearing larger than normal, full and orange like a jewel suspended in the night sky, looking over the population who lay asleep, oblivious to what is happening beneath them.

The ground starts to rumble, within seconds, there is an almighty *crack* sound and chaos instantly falls on to the city. The noise is deafening, screams can be heard from all directions.

Brelos stumbles his way over to the bird cage as chunks of the ceiling shower down on him, the floor moving from under his feet. He falls while simultaneously grabbing the cage, the pigeon squawking and flapping its wings in a panic.

Brelos releases the pigeon, throwing it towards the window. The lintel collapses as the pigeon swoops underneath, to avoid the stone and rubble. Flying down to street level, rubble appears to fall from all directions, clipping the pigeon and sending it crashing to the ground, dead.

Brelos is relieved the message has gone, unaware that the pigeon has not made it out of the city. Brelos makes haste and looks to get to safety. He makes it out on to the street covered in dust; he shakes his head and wipes his eyes. As he manages to open his eyes, he observes the chaos. A man, partly buried by rubble with his legs pinned by the fallen pillar, yelling and screaming for help.

Woman and children are leaving their homes covered in blood from head injuries from fallen debris. A woman is on her knees cradling her dead child. Suddenly, the ground opens spewing out dust and debris, when the dust settles, both mother and child are gone.

Brelos hurry's over to the man pinned by the pillar. 'Please, please, help me, Sir. I beg you!' the man shouts, clinging on to life.

Brelos reaches out, as if helping the man, before rising with a large piece of stone above his head. The man's eyes widen in terror, 'No, Ple…' The man's plea for help cut short, as Brelos slams the piece of stone down on to his head, splattering Brelos's feet and shins with brain matter.

Brelos proceeds through the streets and chaos, fighting his way through the crowds of mass panic. He observes individual's taking advantage of the chaos to rob others of their belongings, woman being raped and children left alone, screaming for their parents that lay crushed beneath the piles of rubble.

Abruptly, Brelos is pushed to the ground as a crowd of Helot's carrying makeshift blades, swords and spears trample over him, killing and slashing at anything in front of them. Brelos quickly crawls out of sight and observes the increasing number of Helot's flooding the streets, creating chaos on top of chaos. Some men stand their ground successfully; others are struck down, arms, legs and head severed from their bodies. It has become clear, the Helots have been planning this revolt for some time and are taking advantage of the earthquake, bringing Sparta to its knees. The Helot's show no mercy, even leaving the women to bleed out in the streets, a murderous revolt.

Brelos continues to observe with a smirk on his face, he has received many payments of coin and gold from Athens for his frequent betrayals.

An ideal situation presents itself to Brelos. He must kill the King amongst all the chaos, knowing the blame will be put on the Helot revolt. With the King removed, political pressures will increase and the heir to the throne will be challenged, as brothers' Cleomenes and Dorieus do not see eye to eye.

Brelos dangerously navigates his way back through the city, making his way to the King's premises. Buildings continue to fall, narrowly missing Brelos and forcing him to change direction.

A Helot appears above Brelos, standing on top of the rubble and covered in the blood of innocent women and children. The Helot points his sword at Brelos and shouts, 'Savrellos, that is my name, I honour you with knowing the name of the slave that will end your life, the last name you will ever hear!'

He leaps off the rubble towards Brelos, who is unarmed. Brelos catches Savrellos slamming him on to his back, swiftly shifting his body into a position of advantage and disarming the Helot with ease.

'I am Brelos, the last name you will ever hear,' Brelos says, pointing the sword at his face. Brelos strikes the Helot, instantly removing the top half of his head; he wipes the sword clean and moves on.

The Helot's have started setting fire to the buildings as the city starts to fill with a thick black smoke, gradually blotting out the orange glow of the moon and replaced with the orange glow of flames. The earthquake eases off, leaving the fate of the shattered city in the Helot's hands, or so it seemed.

A Large group of Helot's gathers, chanting, as if they have led a successful revolt. A Helot slave who appears to be leading the revolt, stands on a large stone to use as a platform to address his people. 'Sparta, the city with no walls, has fallen!'

'Our warriors are the walls!' one Helot sarcastically shouts from the crowd, received with laughter.

'Where are your warriors now, Sparta? You should have built those walls!' the Helot leading the revolt thrusts his sword into the air, encouraging the crowd to do the same. The cheers get louder as the smoke and flames continue to burn the city behind their leader.

Suddenly, a distant chant can be heard. The Helots start to notice as it becomes louder. Gradually, they fall silent to listen to the approaching chants. As it gets louder, they hear the chants along with the banging of shields.

The Helot leader turns around; he is unable to see anything through the smoke, squinting to focus on any movement.

Out of the smoke a pike slams into the chest of the Helot leader, lifting him off his feet and sending him crashing into the crowd. The Helots are looking on in fear to see who is approaching. 'It's a Spartan!' one of the Helot shouts.

A lone figure gradually appears from the smoke as if emerging from the underworld, creating a silhouette with no facial features, just a black empty space when looking at where his eyes should be. The figure yields a sword and shield with the distinct crest upon the helmet, it was Tiro.

Another figure emerges, and then another, and another. More appear until an entire flank of Spartans is in formation. Some of the Helot's decide not to wait around for the retaliation and run. Some of them struck down by other Helot's for being cowards. The Spartans have returned, and they want their city back.

The Spartan's remained in tight formation, shields locked together, spears directed towards their enemy. Their chant continued perfectly in sync with their feet, slowly marching forwards, forcing the Helots to gather closer together.

As the Spartans approached the first line of Helot slaves, they struck them hard and fast, so fast they barely made a sound as dozens of Helots fell lifelessly to the floor, in one swift attack.

The ones who are brave enough to attack the Spartan flanks are instantly dismissed. They are no match for the superior Spartans.

Panic now runs through the remaining Helot's, who start to scatter in all directions. However, they underestimated the Spartans who have already placed ranks in various directions, waiting for the inevitable cowardice of the Helots to set in as they try to retreat. Each one, simultaneously being struck down with ease.

The Spartan's show no mercy as they continue to press upon the revolt, stomping their way through the blood-soaked streets, spearing any Helot survivor clinging onto what life they have left.

Tiro bellows out to the surviving slaves. 'Most of the revolt is now surrounded and a very harsh lesson is about to be taught, and we are your teachers. Forward!'

The Spartans shouted in celebration, as their chant continues to echo through the remains of their city.

'Leave no survivors!' Tiro shouts, taking charge of the attack.

The Spartans are in an exceptional position of advantage and decide to break ranks to fight one on one, enjoying and savouring the moment.

Swiftly they moved on the balls of their feet, arms and legs perfectly positioned and poised, striking hard and fast, with many Spartans deciding not to use their weapons, but to pummel them to death with nothing but their fists and elbows.

Leonidas slices the lower legs from underneath a Helot, sending him to the ground with an almighty *thud.* He finishes him off by crushing his skull with a single stomp to the head, leaving him unrecognisable and disfigured in just two moves.

The thick smoke that engulfs the city begins to disperse, allowing the moon to light up the city floor for its final time before the sun rises.

The Spartans finish off the few that lay breathing before taking a moment to step back and observe the smoldering, shattered remains of their city. The moon providing just enough light to see the level of devastation.

'What shall we do with the dead?' Alec asks out loud.

'Eat them!' Cleombrotus jokingly suggests.

'I wouldn't feed them to the wolves.' Giving one of the dead bodies a kick.

Tiro steps forward and leans over to roll one of the bodies into the huge crack, that has opened up in the Earth.

'Why not use them to fill the crack,' he laughs as he proceeds to roll the body over the edge. Tiro observes the body fall, smashing off the sides before disappearing into complete darkness.

'Did anyone hear him hit the bottom?' They all listen, but not a sound.

'There is no bottom where he's going,' replies Alec.

The Spartans wonder the streets looking for survivors, women and children. The faint sound of screams buried beneath the tons of rubble can still be heard and the stench of burning flesh hovers in the air.

Tiro comes across a slave that has the top half of his head cut off, 'It appears we weren't the only ones to fight back,' smirking at the slave's injuries. He looks up and sees something unusual on the ground; it seems peculiar as it's the only one, a dead pigeon. As he approaches the pigeon with its wings splayed out and damaged, he notices the message tied to its leg.

Tiro picks up the pigeon, looking around to see if anyone is watching. He pulls the message off and reads its contents.

His eyebrows drop and his eyes narrow with rage as he removes his helmet from his head, wiping the sweat from his brow and sweeps his long hair away from his face.

'Brelos, what are you up to?' he mutters to himself, putting his helmet back on and storming off, hoping to find if Brelos has survived the revolt. 'I hope he is dead for his sake,' he mumbles.

Meanwhile, Brelos is on the far side of the city, outside the royal household where the King is residing. The earthquake has caused substantial damage right through the east side of the city. As his presence is known around the house, Brelos hopes for easy access to the King, an opportunity to rid the King will not present itself like this again. Brelos will be awarded with riches beyond his wildest dreams.

The guards outside the household are dead, crushed from the walls they once guarded, but Brelos notices one of the guards with deep knife wound, as he precariously enters the house.

As he works his way through the household, he enters the Queen's quarters. 'Stay back!' shouts a Helot slave and his comrade. They hold the Queen and her servant hostage, looking for anything valuable to steal.

'Brelos, please help us,' the Queen says, with a sense of desperation.

'Help you? I no longer serve the house of Agiad; kill her for all I care, slave. I am here for the King.'

'Ok. He's in there, dead,' the slave points a shocked but happy Brelos to the next room.

'Dead, you say?'

'Yes.'

Brelos looked confused for a moment, 'Why would you kill the King and delay in killing the Queen?'

'We didn't kill the King; he was murdered before we even got here, before the earthquake.'

'What? Impossible!' Brelos could not believe his luck. He walks into the next room; the King's body is lying lifeless on the bed. He looked untouched except for the blood coming out of his ear. Brelos took a closer look and noticed a thin blade had been put through the King's skull via his ear, possibly in his sleep, as there are no signs of a struggle.

'Well, that was unexpected, but it saves me killing the useless bastard,' he shouts to the slaves in the next room. There was a strange silence in the house and Brelos could feel the hairs on the back of his neck stand on end. He turns around; in front of him is Tiro, dirty, covered in blood. Tiro flicks his sword to remove the blood that drips off the tip of his blade, splattering the painted white wall.

Brelos remains silent, not entirely sure what he does or doesn't know. He leans to the left and observes the two slaves on the floor, both with their throats slit.

The Queen and her servant get up to leave, the Queen approaches Tiro, 'The man before you murdered your King. You know what to do.'

Tiro nods and signals for the Queen to leave. 'We need to find Cleomenes and Dorieus,' she says to her servant, as they turn and leave.

'You killed my Father and the King, traitorous bastard.' Tiro is poised and ready to end Brelos's life.

'Well, that's not entirely true, I have no idea who killed the King, he was dead before the earthquake, I'm sure of it. Cicero is alive and well, he is with the others.'

'You know damn well that's not who I am referring to, I've figured it out. The body, the sneaking around and deals you have made with my so-called Father!'

'Oh, ok, so what? What now, you just kill everyone that has given you a life worth living? You're a warrior, not some half-starved peasant.'

'Yes, in a nut shell.'

'Then kill Cicero, he's as much as a traitor as I am,' Brelos said with a sense of arrogance, confident he can talk his way out of the situation.

Tiro loosens the grip on his sword and widens his stance slightly, just enough to transfer his energy from his feet through to his hips.

'Brelos, do us both a favour and shut your mouth.' He lunges forward aggressively.

Brelos quickly shifts out of the way, surprising Tiro with his nimbleness.

'Not bad old man,' says Tiro, tilting his head from left to right to release his tight neck muscles, making his neck click.

Brelos twists from the hips, releasing a *'crack'* in his back. Realising Tiro is determined to see this fight through, he leans over to the King, sliding the blade out of his skull. Both are now armed.

'C'mon Tiro, what are you waiting for, permission?' Brelos tosses the blade from one hand to another.

'Are you ready to die?' replies Tiro.
Brelos responds with an awkward smile, 'fuck you.'

8

The dry foliage between the houses that also borders much of Sparta's streets, burns furiously. It spreads rapidly as the breeze provides the flames with life; the houses quickly start to fill with smoke. Brelos and Tiro are silent and the time for talking is over, someone must die.

Tiro throws down his blade, he decides Brelos is not worthy of such a clean death and wants to deliver a more painful, slower death. Brelos uses this opportunity to his advantage, plunging at Tiro.

Quickly countered, Tiro plants his elbow into his jaw. Brelos stumbles, wiping the blood from his lips with the back of his hand.

Brelos is aggressive and no stranger to violence. He initiates another attack, avoiding Tiro's counter move and slicing his blade across Tiro's shoulder.

Tiro makes a small grunt acknowledging his wound, fortunately not deep enough to slow him down.

Brelos picks up Tiro's sword, 'Well, if you're not going to use it,' Brelos says, shrugging his shoulders before charging at him again. Brelos, the clear aggressor.

Tiro ducked beneath the first swipe, pivots around the next plunge while grabbing Brelos's wrists. Slamming Brelos into the wall, flames from the burning shrubs creep over the window edge. Tiro has the strength to secure Brelos while using his other hand to force Brelos's face towards the flames.

Brelos starts to scream as the flames tickle the side of his face, his hair catches fire but Tiro is too strong and his skin starts to burn, blistering from the heat.

Brelos drops the sword and receives Tiro's knee, driven into his sternum. Brelos drops to one knee.

Tiro slams Brelos's head into the wall, splitting the ridge of his nose. Blood gushes up the wall and down his face as he falls onto his back. Tiro proceeds to stamp on his chest before climbing on top of him and driving his fist into his face, breaking the eye socket.

Brelos was barely conscious, both eyes badly swollen, cut and burnt. Tiro forces him to stand up, 'I'm not finished with you yet!'

Brelos makes a naïve attempt to swing for Tiro, falling over from his own momentum.

'Stand up!' Tiro shouts, throwing Brelos against the wall as he presses his forearm against his chest to keep him standing. He repeatedly punches his torso, until the majority of Brelos's ribs are broken.

Brelos coughs up blood, wheezing uncontrollably, he desperately gasps for air clutching at his stomach in agony.

Tiro steps back with a smile to enjoy observing Brelos slowly suffering, his life slowly slipping away from him. Brelos tries to pick up the small blade that killed the King with the intention to end his own suffering.

'Once a coward, always a coward,' says Tiro, shaking his head in disbelief. Tiro kicks the blade away from Brelos and makes a single swipe with his sword, removing Brelos's arm. It was removed so quickly Brelos barely noticed. *Swoosh!* Tiro removes the other arm; Brelos is on his knees slumped, armless and trembling from the shock. Tiro places his sword under Brelos's chin to lift his head, 'You won't need those arms where you're going, old man,' he says looking into his partially closed eye.

Brelos uses every ounce of energy to make a slight smirk, knowing this is his last moment, alive.

Swoosh! Tiro removes Brelos's head with a single swipe of his sword. His head rolls off his body, landing in to the vast pool of blood surrounding his twitching corpse, blood squirting over Tiro's shins and feet as it spurts from his severed veins.

The room is now full of thick smoke and Tiro needs to leave the house fast, pausing to look at the King on his way out. A few minutes pass, Tiro exits the house cradling the King, gently placing him down on to the ground.

The Queen returns with Cleomenes and Dorieus by her side, they hurry over to where the King rests. 'What happened?' says Dorieus, as he kneels down to see the King.

Tiro steps to the side bowing his head in respect, allowing them space.

Cleomenes is silent, his facial expression blank, not knowing how to deal with the situation. Suddenly he lets out a single loud scream of despair, looking up to the sky in disbelief.

'He was murdered by Brelos,' says Tiro out loud.

'Did you say Brelos?' says Dorieus, as he stands to face Tiro.

'I don't believe you. How could you know that?' Cleomenes shakes his head in disbelief.

'It's true I walked in on him standing over the King. Brelos said he was already dead but I didn't believe him for a moment!' the Queen says interrupting the others.

Dorieus looks around at the chaos surrounding him. 'Where's Brelos now?'

'He's in there. Well, what's left of him,' Tiro replies, nodding his head towards the door.

Dorieus and Cleomenes walk in to the building crouching low and covering their mouths to avoid inhaling the smoke. Several moments later they reappear.

'Shit. You did some fine work in there, Tiro. I do not understand why Brelos would turn on our Father, but he got what he deserved,' Dorieus says.

'Athens will love this! They'll take full advantage of these events!' stresses Cleomenes, shaking his head.

'Athens do not need to find out the King was murdered; we will say it was from natural causes. Brelos was a traitor, spying for Athens! They will not hear back from him and assume he was caught and killed,' Tiro says, frustrated.

'Fuck! Did he admit this? If so, you can guarantee he has already sent a message to Athens, so much for the fucking truce!' Cleomenes says, cursing to himself.

Tiro held up the pigeon's message. 'You're right, he did send a message but it didn't get very far. I found this on a dead messenger pigeon, hence how I knew the King was in danger. Unfortunately, I was too late to save the King.' Tiro bows his head while Dorieus places his hand on his shoulder.

'Head high, Spartan. You avenged the King's death, my Father's death, our Father's death. So, thank you.'

Tiro gives a single nod. As he turns away, he notices Leonidas and Cleombrotus approaching.

'Our Father is dead!' shouted Cleomenes.

Leonidas and Cleombrotus simultaneously look at each other.

'Murdered by Brelos, who was spying for Athens. Fortunately, Tiro arrived, ultimately saving the Queen and avenged our Father's death,' Dorieus says, pointing to Tiro who has since taken a seat on a large piece of stone rubble.

The remaining troops begin to congregate around Leonidas and Cleombrotus, bowing their heads when noticing their dead King.

Leonidas pulls Cleombrotus to one side in private. 'Well, I must admit, I wasn't expecting Brelos to take the blame so easily, but I'll accept it none the less,' Leonidas says, with little remorse.

'We stick to the long-term plan brother; our city and our country will be better off. Killing our Father was the easy part. I didn't hesitate and if anything, I put him out of his misery. Sparta comes first,' explains Cleombrotus, reassuring himself.

They both embrace, Leonidas observes Tiro over Cleombrotus's shoulder. 'We need rid of Cicero next, otherwise he will be a thorn in our side,' suggests Leonidas.

Cleombrotus turns to observe Tiro. 'I'm confident he can get the job done; tensions are high between them both by all accounts.'

Leonidas approaches Tiro, who still remains seated slouched over and resting his elbow on his thigh, pinching the bridge of his nose between his thumb and finger. His eyes are closed and he takes a lungful of air before exhaling in a drawn-out sigh.

'You look troubled, something on your mind, brother?' Leonidas asks, leaning under Tiro slightly to attract his attention.

Leonidas brushes off some rubble fragments and takes a seat besides Tiro; encouraging Tiro to lean to one side.

'I have something I need to tell you Leonidas, I am not sure you are going to like what you hear,' Tiro says, lifting his head to face Leonidas.

'Try me, I don't think today can get any worse to be honest with you.'

Tiro takes his time putting his words together and is partially distracted as the remaining citizens and Spartans collect the wounded, trapped beneath the rubble.

'We've established Brelos was informing the Athenians of our activity, if the message had made it to Athens we would be under attack within the next few days, we would be extremely vulnerable,' Tiro explains, with a concerned expression.

'Yes Tiro, fortunately for Sparta it has the likes of you and I for walls and we would fight every single one of them until our last breath. Is it this that bothers you, Tiro?'

'No, I fear I could have prevented this as I have had some concerns about my Father, I have reason to believe he is involved. Looking back on recent events it suddenly pieces together. Confidential meetings with Brelos, suspicious behavior, it makes sense now. Brelos would not have done this on his own, he would need a position of power supporting his cause,' Tiro says, increasingly getting angrier the longer he discusses it.

'There's something else on your mind, isn't there?'

'Yes, Leonidas, and I don't know what will happen to me if what I know, becomes common knowledge. I will be spat on by our fellow comrades,' Tiro says, frustratingly.

Leonidas stands up and looks over Tiro, flicking his red cloak behind him and placing his hands on his hips, making a stance of authority. 'You have my word Tiro, you will not be disregarded,' Leonidas says, in a firm voice.

Tiro cautiously looks around before telling Leonidas what he knows, he trusted Leonidas impeccably.

'Cicero is not my Father; they couldn't have children so they stole me, raising me as their own. It's no wonder the God's wouldn't allow them to be with child,' Tiro says, looking in to Leonidas's eyes for some kind of reaction. Leonidas couldn't believe his luck, he had plans to put a level of blame on Cicero for the death of the King, but Cicero had made it easy for him.

'Well, shit! I wasn't expecting that,' replies Leonidas, as he folds his arms, shaking his head in disbelief.

'There's more. That body we came across.'

'I remember. The remains of the slave the wolves finished off. What of it?'

'That was no slave Leonidas, that was my real Father who had found me that evening and explained where I was from. Brelos had been ordered to track him down and murder him by my Father, I mean Cicero. He didn't want me to find out and disgrace his name and jeopardise his position as an Ephor.'

Leonidas remains silent, in disbelief.

'That's why I had no concerns about butchering Brelos in there today, it was personal. Cicero knows that I know the truth,' Tiro says, clenching his blood-stained fists.

Leonidas paces a few strides to the left, then to the right, thinking of his next move. He needs Cicero gone, but as an Ephor it would be impossible to prove what Tiro knows.

Leonidas pauses for a moment. Stroking his chin, he senses the anger and frustrating coming from Tiro. He places a hand on Tiro's shoulder and whispers in to his ear.

'Tiro, you know what you need to do my friend. This ends here with us; nobody will ever know.'

Tiro sits himself up straight and becomes more assertive, he is taken back by the loyalty Leonidas displays before him.

'Deal with this Tiro, but discretely. If you get caught, I can't help you, so I suggest you do it promptly under the cover of darkness. It wouldn't be unrealistic to think he fell down one of these cracks would it? Look at the state of the city now, we will lose many by sunrise,' Leonidas suggests, widening his eyes and raising his eyebrows.

Tiro couldn't understand why Leonidas would hint at the assassination of an Ephor, regardless of wrong doings. However, Tiro didn't question his thought process and knew in his gut, this is what he wanted.

'Your so-called Father is poison Tiro and Sparta has no room for such deceit.'

Cleombrotus approaches them both. Tiro uses this as a reason to end the conversation. Leonidas gives Tiro a nod of approval and walks away with Cleombrotus.

'How did your little chat go, brother?' Cleombrotus asks, with a sense of reservation.

'Not as expected, but surprisingly well brother, surprisingly well.'

'Ok,' shrugging his shoulders, having trust in his brother's judgment.

Sparta still burns, it is kept under control by surviving Helot slaves stamping out the flames before they take control. This creates excess amounts of thick black smoke that fills the night sky, partially hiding the moon.

Distant screams can still be heard with the occasional crashing noise of masonry thudding on to the ground around Tiro, as he walks through the city to locate Cicero.

Tiro moves quickly, conscious of how much cover of darkness remains before sunrise. He pulls his cloak across his face to prevent breathing in the thick smoke, despite still being able to smell it through the material, causing him to cough and splutter.

It's not long before Tiro finds himself on the trail leading to Cicero's house. It is on a slight incline built in to the hill side, looking over the roof tops of the houses below. As Tiro approaches, he pauses as he notices Cicero fumbling around outside, gathering his things together. Tiro steps out in front of him. Cicero, startled to see him.

'Tiro, I didn't see you there!' Cicero says, out of breath and confused.

Tiro responds with a clean punch straight to the mouth of Cicero, knocking out his two front teeth. Cicero's head snaps back from the power of Tiro's punch as the blood spills down his chin. Falling on to his back, his head crashing on to the stony ground, instantly rendering him unconscious.

There was not much time, Tiro remained composed as he sticks to the plan, conjured on his walk over to the house. He wraps Cicero in his red cloak, making sure it covers his face so nobody would recognise who it was. Tiro slings him over his shoulder with ease, hoping anyone seeing him carrying a body would assume Tiro was recovering a body, from the evening's disaster.

Despite feeling tired after the events of the night, Tiro wastes no time making his way toward Mount Taygetus. The climb quickly becomes steep and Tiro's breathing becomes laboured, but his sheer strength and determination allow him to keep climbing.

Cicero begins to move slightly, Tiro approaches the edge of the mountain known to be where unfit Spartan babies are discarded.

Tiro dumps him on to the ground as he drops to one knee to catch his breath, using his forearm to wipe the sweat from his brow.

The air has become much cooler, the view provides a chance for Tiro to see the true extent of the chaos, as he observes the orange glow over Sparta. A layer of thick black smoke above the city moves slowly across the horizon as the wind rolling down the mountains encourages the smoke to travel across the landscape.

Cicero begins to stir and groan before opening his eyes, wiping the blood from his chin; he puts his fingers in his mouth and realises his teeth are missing. Looking around he can only see darkness; he sits up and see's Tiro standing before him. 'Where the hell am I?'

'Shut up, traitor.'

Cicero knows he is about to see his end and is thinking fast to somehow resolve the situation. He is a fit man but he is no match for Tiro. Tiro on a bad day would still be a challenge. Cicero stands himself up looking over his shoulder and realises he is backed on to a steep ledge. 'Ok, Ok Tiro, I know what this is but this is not the answer, I am an Ephor! People will ask where I am, can you not see that; how would you explain this?'

Tiro shrugs his shoulders. 'You will not need to worry about that where you are going.'

Cicero suddenly felt an overwhelming sense of fear, something he has not felt in a long time. 'Son, listen to me.'

'I am not your son, Cicero!'

'Tiro, what happened to Orien needed to be done and you wouldn't have known any different if he hadn't found you.'

Tiro was starting to lose his patience, he pushes Cicero forcing him to stumble on to one knee.

'You have a brother, Tiro. Born the summer after we took you, I know his name and location.'

'I'm not interested, this makes no difference to me or your fate! Stand up and face your end, like a man!'

Cicero stands as he comes to terms with his inevitable end, shaking his head in disbelief. Tiro forces him to turn around and leans him beyond the cliff edge while holding on to his garment. 'Tiro, my only request is to allow me to face you, I will not struggle, you have my word.'

Tiro pauses for a moment, taking a deep breath. He observes the suns glow break the night sky over the horizon, as day light begins to rise slowly over the city. He closes his eyes just for a moment, exhales and calmly replies, 'No!'

Cicero peers over his shoulder. 'Your brother isn't like you Tiro, his name is Artabanus and he resides in Persia.'

Tiro releases his grip; anticipating his fall, Cicero turns to look in to Tiro's eyes. He falls without making a sound and without breaking eye contact, until his body smashes off the mountain side. His body smashes off another ledge, propelling his mangled body over the final edge, into darkness.

The distant cry of a wolf echoes through the valley. The sun continues to rise releasing an intense beam breaking over the horizon, casting through the valley and lighting up the mountain side. With his eyes closed, Tiro embraces the warmth of the sun light as it moves up his body and over his face. He turns and follows the path back to the city, but with the death of the King and a city in despair, Tiro senses more is yet to come.

9

The morning sun shines intensely over Sparta, the heat already uncomfortable. What looks like a morning mist hovering above the streets is in fact the smoldering remains of a fractured city.

The remaining Helot slaves are under control, under the watchful eye of Spartans. Those who have taken the opportunity to try and flee the city have been struck down before they can succeed. Women and children are being treated for their wounds and burns and provided whatever food and water is available, by Spartan women.

Despite the velocity of the earthquake, much of the city remains standing. The earthquake had mainly devastated the east side of the city that is predominantly populated with the Helot population.

Leonidas and Cleombrotus have returned to their royal household, it has sustained substantial damage. However, it remains standing.

The household servants have already cleaned up Brelos's remains and the guard Cleombrotus murdered to eliminate the chances of eye witnesses. The second guard still remains under the fallen wall.

Servants are now in the process of prepping the King's body. The city's population is not yet aware of the King's death but the council will need to convene quickly, before the news breaks.

Leonidas ushers Cleombrotus to a secluded part of the house where they can talk, without interference.

Leonidas double checks nobody is around to listen in, 'My brother, we need to check that Tiro has dealt with Cicero. If he has, everything is going to plan, despite a few surprises.'

Cleombrotus nods in agreement, 'Yes, the important thing is, there is no suspicion linked to either of us.'

'We stick to the bigger, long-term plan. If we are correct in our way of thinking, then the council will appoint Cleomenes as the King of the Agiad dynasty,' Leonidas says, confidently.

'How are you so sure they do not appoint Dorieus?'

'Brother, Cleomenes is a natural tactician and his abilities far exceed Dorieus. The council will favour this, especially with our fragile relationship with Athens. The two of them clash, Dorieus will likely protest and leave the city on other ventures, which is what we want. He's practically said as much in the past! The fact remains, Cleomenes is the first born.'

'You're right, Leonidas. Cleomenes is an excellent tactician but he doesn't have what it takes to be King. You do, I am willing to die for that cause.'

'Thank you, brother, but let's hope that won't be necessary as I need you by my side as my senior advisor. We are both young and must remain patient.'

'Agreed,' Cleombrotus says, as they both firmly grip arms and embrace. Their bond was strong, but to climb to the top and lead Sparta they will need to trust each other like never before and learn all there is to know.

The day progresses quickly, the afternoon heat continues to beat down on to the city creating an uncomfortable level of humidity.

The Gerousia spent the morning discussing a plan of action on appointing a new King of the Agiad dynasty, and what is to be told to the population regarding the death of Anaxandridas.

The council requests the presence of King Demaratus of the Eurypontid dynasty, an unpopular successor to Ariston. It is rumoured Demaratus is not the son of Ariston but that of Agetus, his mother's first husband.

Cleomenes, Dorieus, Leonidas and Cleombrotus are all in attendance, the tension between Cleomenes and Dorieus could be cut with a knife.

Cleomenes appeared smug, knowing it is highly likely the Gerousia will confirm his new position as the King, because he is directly inline to the throne, being the first born.

Dorieus always held a grudge for being the second born to his Father's first wife. Dorieus believes this should be taken in to account but he knows it is customary in Sparta for the first born to be inline.

The Gerousia is an intimate building, semi-circular with two rows of twenty pillars, supporting a terracotta tiled roof providing a shaded area over part of the seating. The seating was similar in style to an amphitheater, surrounding a raised circular platform on ground level, where the senior Spartan of the Gerousia would present to the council. Hanging in the center, above the seating, three large red banners display the letter lambda in gold, standing for Lacedaemon.

Surrounding the perimeter are cypress trees, thirty feet in height. Across the entrance are six pillars with a wide opening in the middle, allowing access on to the cobbled stone pathway that was always guarded by six Spartan soldiers, three either side.

The members of the Gerousia assemble. Taking their seats, they start discussions among themselves on why they are there. The Gerousia was built to enhance acoustics for the lead speaker. As a result, as voices echo through the building the conversations merge in to a single droning noise.

'Let's proceed, gentlemen,' says a bellowing voice, echoing through the hall from a Spartan elder called Lycurgus. The most senior Spartan in the Gerousia.

'You are aware of why we are here today; our great leader and King is dead! Betrayed and murdered by his trusted helping hand, Brelos!' Murmurs travel throughout the Gerousia and Lycurgus raises both arms in the air, indicating for silence. The council obliges.

All the brothers are sitting in the front row and Dorieus has made the point of sitting on the opposite side to Cleomenes.

Both Cleombrotus and Leonidas are sat in the middle, separating the two.

Lycurgus continues, 'Fortunately, justice was swiftly served by Spartan, Tiro, who intercepted Brelos. Unfortunately, it was too late for the King. We shall erect a monument in his memory for generations to see.' The majority of the council nod their heads in agreement, some giving a cheer of approval.

The Queen, mother of Cleomenes, walks in to the Gerousia. The council stands as a sign of respect. Lycurgus has his back to the Queen and has not realised she has entered, he turns and see's the Queen before him, bowing his head to address her appropriately.

'Please precede, Lycurgus,' the Queen says, as she steps to the side to observe the council.

Lycurgus turns to readdress the council, noticing a smirk on Leonidas's face; Leonidas knows she has arrived to see her son become the new King of the Agiad dynasty.

Lycurgus demands the council to stand, calling for Cleomenes to present himself. 'Cleomenes of the Agiad dynasty, priest of Zeus, you are presented here today to the council of our glorious city of Sparta, and the Eurypontid dynasty, as the first born of King Anaxandridas II.' Cleomenes has a smug look on his face as he focuses his attention on Dorieus, having great satisfaction seeing Dorieus's despair.

Lycurgus continues, 'The Gerousia officially announces you, Sparta's King Cleomenes the 1st of the Agiad dynasty.'
Dorieus stands abruptly, 'This is ridiculous, a mistake, why can't any of you see that?' Cleombrotus grabs his arm to try and encourage Dorieus to sit back down.

'Brother, you are making a fool of yourself and the house of Agiad.'

'Sit down, boy!' Shouts Lycurgus, partially spitting over Dorieus in the process.

'No, Sir, I will not, it is not my intention to disrespect the Gerousia and its members, but I will not sit here and pretend you are doing the right thing simply based on the fact

Cleomenes was born first. I was born to the true, original Queen of Sparta, learning much of my Father's ways.' Some members of the council gasp in disbelief at Dorieus's comment, while others curse him and demand he leaves the Gerousia.

Lycurgus calls the guards to escort Dorieus from the Gerousia, Dorieus barges through them with his shoulder before they have a chance to handle him. The Gerousia erupts in angry conversation as it echoes around the building, Lycurgus demands for order and silence, getting back to the needs of Sparta.

Once the council finished their discussions, Cleombrotus and Leonidas go in search for Dorieus. They eventually find him back at their Father's household, leaning over the body of Anaxandridas that is laying prepared for the burial, that is due to take place the following morning.

Leonidas doesn't mix his words. 'What the fuck was that, brother? You've just single handedly shamed the Agiad dynasty, not only that, but you did it in front of the entire council, including the fucking Eurypontid dynasty!'

'You know Cleomenes doesn't have the knowledge I have Leonidas; he barely spent any time around our Father during childhood. He was always with his mother in a different household!'

Cleombrotus steps forward with a suggestion, 'You need to leave brother; the council want you banished, from Sparta.'

'Did they suggest that?' replied Dorieus, concerned with the potential outcome of his outburst. Cleombrotus nudges Leonidas to encourage him to play along.

'Yes, that's right Dorieus, now they know you do not support their cause they see you as a threat to Cleomenes.'

Dorieus starts to pace around the room, scratching his head and stroking his chin as he slips into deep thought. 'What would you suggest?'

'Beat them to it brother, make the suggestion before they have the chance,' suggests Cleombrotus.

'Couldn't agree more, play it to your advantage brother, with your knowledge you could start your own colony that would rival any other,' Leonidas says, firmly patting Dorieus on the back. By the look on Dorieus's face he was starting to believe in his potential as a leader with some gentle persuasion.

'They are having another meeting tomorrow after the King's burial to undoubtedly discuss how they are going to act on your outburst. You chose a really bad time to air your frustrations brother.'

Dorieus steps between his brothers, placing his arms around their shoulders. 'Thank you, both, I will put my plan together tonight and address the council tomorrow.'

Leonidas and Cleombrotus simultaneously nod in agreement and leave. As they walk away Leonidas stops, noticing something in his peripheral vision, Tuto.

The white owl was perched on a nearby tree branch. Rotating its head, it looks straight at Leonidas before leaping from the branch, flying out of sight. Leonidas saw this as a good sign and was confident tomorrow would see his brother Dorieus leaving Sparta, one way or another.

The following day, there is a sense of mourning throughout Sparta, the former King had a long and successful reign and was respected highly among the elders.

He was buried with no headstone, which is not unusual in Sparta, only those who die in battle are given headstones that merely state 'In War,' no name and no dates. To have such a headstone placed upon a grave is considered the greatest honour for a Spartan warrior.

The majority who attended the burial make their way straight to the Gerousia to discuss arrangements around Dorieus, and his outburst.

The council assembles with Dorieus and his brothers in attendance, with Lycurgus heading the meeting. Lycurgus could see Dorieus was keen to speak, but he wouldn't dare interrupt again.

'Care to speak, Dorieus? I can't carry on while you sit there fidgeting, get whatever it is off your chest.'

Dorieus was surprised he was given the opportunity. 'Yes, I would like to make a suggestion,' Dorieus announced nervously, as he precedes to stand in front of the council. 'Firstly, I did not intend to insult the council with my outburst or the Spartan traditions that have been in place for hundreds of years. I have had time to cool off and respect the decision that has been made,' Dorieus explains, telling them what they want to hear, rather than what he actually thinks.

'Precede,' says Lycurgus, making a gesture with his hand to continue.

'Thank you. Despite the fact I have accepted the decision, I simply cannot remain in Sparta under the reign of Cleomenes, I won't!'

'Well, what do you suggest?' one of the elders asks.

There was a moment of silence as the council waited in anticipation to hear Dorieus's suggestion.

'I want to be granted a body of men, enough for me to establish a settlement of my own under my leadership. Dorieus knew of many Spartan men who would prefer to follow under his leadership.

The elders began to talk among themselves while others laughed off the suggestion, Lycurgus demanded order.

'Where do you intend to settle Dorieus?'

'I am thinking the Tripolitania region. Cinyps. to be more precise.'

After much debate, the council decide to grant Dorieus with his wish, including a selection of men to accompany him.

'Sparta grants you with your men and ambitions, only upon agreement from the Delphic Oracle, before you intend to depart,' Lycurgus demands.

Dorieus gives the nod of his head, 'I will travel to Delphi at first light, tomorrow.'

Later that afternoon, Leonidas and Cleombrotus approach Dorieus who has already gathered his belongings as if planning to leave immediately. Leonidas looks surprised to see Dorieus so well organised, 'You are leaving now, brother?'

'Yes, shortly before the sun falls so my men and I can travel in cooler conditions and under darkness, to avoid the elders.'

'You don't intend to consult the Oracle, do you, brother?' Cleombrotus asks.

Dorieus stops what he is doing, turning to face Cleombrotus. 'I will not consult anyone any further, my men are ready to go at a moment's notice and I will not let the Oracle dictate to me. From now on, I do things my way!' Dorieus begins to become agitated the more he discusses the situation with his brothers. He peers outside to observe the suns position to help judge what time he has left before leaving.

Leonidas encourages Dorieus to leave at the earliest opportunity. 'I recommend you leave now, brother. Especially if you are going against the council's agreement to consult the Oracle. They will not take kindly to that decision; you must leave now!'

The twins usher Dorieus to quickly gather his things and make way to meet his men on the outskirts of Sparta. 'You are right, brothers, I must leave now.' Convinced, Dorieus makes haste, embraces his brothers and leaves Sparta.

The twin brothers observe Dorieus as he disappears over the horizon that begins to fall under darkness as the sun quickly begins to set. They turn and look at one another smiling.

'One less obstacle, my brother' - patting Cleombrotus on the back - 'Now I must inform the council Dorieus has left without consulting the Oracle, purely to reinforce their rapidly growing disappointment in him.'

10

Since the council was informed of Dorieus's premature departure, it's back to business for the elders as today marks the day of a new kingship. The introduction of King Cleomenes of the Agiad dynasty and Demaratus, King of the Eurypontid dynasty.

Despite both rule Sparta in partnership, there has always been a frosty relationship between the two houses. The Agiad dynasty has always been favoured and looked upon as more superior. Demaratus has voiced his opinions about this in the past, therefore; it is no surprise that Cleomenes has already done his research on Demaratus.

Cleomenes is already well known for being a great tactician and there is no doubt he is already one step ahead of Demaratus.

Everyone is in attendance and Lycurgus asks everyone to be seated so they can start. 'So, we are here today for the official introduction of the two Kings and to discuss the relationship between Sparta and Athens. After the death of your Father Cleomenes, our King, this relationship and treaty is fractured beyond repair and we must demonstrate our dismay.'

'No!' Cleomenes says, abruptly.

The elders are taken back, they assumed after the death of his Father he would be out for vengeance. However, Cleomenes held more composure than expected and he had other intentions on keeping the peace with Athens.

Cleomenes stands to address the council, turning his back on Demaratus in an obvious attempt to boycott him. 'The passing of my Father is already old news in my eyes, his service to Sparta was long, but he failed to maintain a stable relationship with Athens. If we go to war with Athens, we exhaust our resources and a generation of men, unnecessarily.'

Some of the council nod in agreement, and as the new King, he has already started to gain their attention and respect.

'I disagree, we need to show our strength, not kiss their backsides with so called peace talks. They've already demonstrated their lack of adherence to that,' explains a frustrated Demaratus.

One of the elders looks to speak, before being interrupted by Cleomenes. 'If you don't mind, I would like to respond to that statement. Firstly, you have contributed very little to the development and success of Sparta during your reasonably long reign as King, and you have spent most of your time abiding by the decisions made by the Agiad dynasty.'

There is an awkward silence among the elders as they listened to the unexpected response from such a new King.

Demaratus stands to retaliate but is cut off by Cleomenes.

'Secondly, Demaratus, it's no secret that your legitimacy to even be a King is questionable. Ariston, Agetus? I guess we'll never know, for sure! Fancy having a King rule Sparta, that may or may not have a legitimate birth right to the throne.'

As Cleomenes looks around at the elders, he knows by their expression he has just sown the seed of doubt. Despite already knowing this, the elders had always ignored it. However, for Sparta to be taken seriously, Demaratus may not be the right King to lead the Eurypontid dynasty.

Later that day, Cleomenes requests Cleombrotus and Leonidas accompany him to discuss arrangements.

'Can you believe the shame Dorieus has placed on this dynasty? Good riddance to him! However, because of his absence you both need to step up and take the reins. Do you understand, brothers? Cleomenes asks.

'Yes, of course,' both replying, simultaneously.

'What are your plans, Cleomenes? If I know you like I think I do, you have everything planned out already,' says Leonidas.

Suddenly, there is some commotion and shouting. Demaratus storms his way through, shoving Cleomenes with both hands, sending him tumbling over.

'What the fuck are you playing at?' If you are trying to intimidate me it won't work, Cleomenes!' Demaratus shouts, his face turning red with anger.

'This right here, Demaratus, just proves to me you can't handle your role as King. You, are a yes man. My Father was too weak to confront you, but I am not. The moment you feel a bit of pressure and confrontation, you erupt, uncontrollably. Perhaps you can join my useless brother, Dorieus. He could do with some help.'

Demaratus straightens himself out, lifts his chin high and storms off in a temper.

'Well, Leonidas, you can guarantee part of my plan intends to get rid of that useless shit, but something tells me you already knew that,' says Cleomenes, placing his hand on Leonidas's shoulder.

Cleomenes slowly walks off, muttering to himself and stroking his chin, deep in thought.

Leonidas looks puzzled at his behaviour, 'What's wrong, brother?'

'Just a thought, I am going to contact an old friend who reached out to me recently.'

'And who is this old friend, brother?'

Cleomenes Smiles, 'Isagoras.'

Cleombrotus turns to Cleomenes wearing a frown. 'Isagoras, of Athens? That's your plan?'

'Yes, we are well acquainted and he provided me hospitality during my last trip to Athens to force tyrant Hippias out of Athens. I had to take hostage of all the Pisistratidae children, but it worked.'

Isagoras is an Athenian aristocrat, a man of wealth. Very well educated, he believes he is more popular than he actually is among the Athenian people.

'If you are still well acquainted, I am assuming he doesn't know you slept with his wife?' Leonidas laughs, shaking his head in disbelief.

'No, of course he doesn't, but I installed Isagoras at the head of an oligarchy made up of Athenian aristocrats that were loyal or sympathetic to Sparta; leaving Isagoras unrivalled in power within the city. However, Cleisthenes opposed him, and then one of his relatives from the Alcmaeonid clan was elected Chief Archon the following year. Therefore, he requests our intervention. With his position we should be able to establish a better relationship with Athens.'

Leonidas thinks for a moment about his plan, 'Who is this, Cleisthenes?'

Cleomenes shrugs his shoulders, 'He's an Athenian lawgiver and member of the aristocratic Alcmaeonid clan. He is keen to provide Athenian citizens with more power. The majority of Athens, particularly the middle and lower classes, desire a return to democracy. We do not wish to see a democratic Athens, because a free and democratic Athens would be dangerous to Spartan power.'

'So, he has reached out to you to remove Cleisthenes? To me this sounds like a revolt and I don't owe Isagoras a thing!'

Leonidas starts pacing in frustration, scratching his head while trying to make sense of the discussion. Cleomenes can see he is frustrated but is confident he can talk him around.

'Listen, Leonidas, Isagoras is currently up against Cleisthenes. All he needs is our help for one last push to exile him out of Athens, imposing himself again as the new leader of an oligarchy. It's highly likely Cleisthenes will not be a threat and before you know it, we are in favour and return home. This is for Sparta!'

Cleombrotus throws his arms in the air. 'Great, this gets better, brother. What you are basically saying is, you want to invade Athens and hope that this puts Isagoras back in a position of control, over the Athenian people?

'Yes, exactly. With Isagoras in power, this will put Sparta in a much more powerful position. With us by his side, Athens and Sparta will be at peace.'

Leonidas is still unsure; his instincts tell him this is a bad idea but is torn by his brother's ability as a tactician.

Cleombrotus steps forward and puts both his hands-on Leonidas's shoulders, 'Cleomenes might be right. This is the city that wanted our Father and King assassinated, during a truce! Remember, they conspired with Brelos to kill him, do this for Sparta!'

Cleombrotus widens his eyes and nods to Leonidas as a gentle reminder that as far as everyone else is concerned, Brelos is the one who killed the King.

Leonidas nods in agreement, 'Cleomenes, get a message to Isagoras. Tell him we are on our way.'

'Already have, brother.'

'You've already agreed without even taking this to the council first?' Leonidas shocked by the statement.

'Don't worry about the council, leave them to me. Isagoras has already rallied a lot of support; fetch two of the finest Spartans to accompany us.'

Cleomenes leaves enthusiastically to approach the council, pleased that his brothers will be supporting him. Cleomenes was confident in his approach and the council did not hesitate to approve their plan.

It is a risk but entering Athens through the back door, but alongside an already powerful Isagoras, it is a great way to get revenge and peace simultaneously. Isagoras has a following of citizens that should be adequate enough to see the plan through.

Cleomenes locates his brothers to inform them of the good news, 'Chosen who will be accompany us yet?'

Leonidas leans back, 'The council have approved it already?'

'Of course, they have, did you doubt me?'

'We will be accompanied by Tiro and Alec, two of our greatest warriors, after me of course.' Cleombrotus can't help but laugh at himself.

'Ok, good, pack your shit together because in two days we are leaving for Athens.'

The Spartans head back to their homes to spend some last-minute quality time, with their loved ones.

Leonidas sighs, 'Here we go.'

11

The journey on horseback was long, hot and uncomfortable. Like much of Greece, the air is dry and the ground is hard. The air was so hot that they could feel their lips burn and their nostrils tingle each time they took a breath.

Within the city walls, Athens was crowded and busy with pop up markets in what seems like every available space, selling anything from jewelry to livestock. In comparison to Sparta, Athens had an overwhelming sense of power and wealth. The sheer scale and precision of the masonry was something they had never seen before. However, Cleomenes was taking it all in his stride, as he had been to Athens before.

Ahead was a steep hillside surrounded by trees, on top was a series of structures and temples that caught Alec's eye as the sunlight reflected brilliantly off the limestone they were constructed from.

'What is that place, up there?' Alec asks, pointing to the top of the hill.

'That's the Acropolis; the large structure is referred to as the old temple. That's dedicated to their patron goddess, Athena,' replies Cleomenes.

Leonidas had never seen such architecture, but Sparta was not interested in colossal structures and temples and in comparison, was very basic.

'No doubt it is perfectly positioned for strategic military defense?' Leonidas says out loud.

'Of course, it is,' replies Cleomenes.

The Spartans remained on the outskirts of the city where Isagoras was planning to meet them, to discuss their plans. It was not long until Cleomenes notices a small group of men up ahead. He immediately recognised his old friend, despite swirls of hot air rising from the ground creating a blurred image.

Isagoras steps forward and embraces Cleomenes. 'Cleomenes, my old friend. Thank you for gracing us with your presence. I truly owe you. My condolences too, news travelled that your Father passed. He was a great leader, warrior and King.'

'Thank you, I hope you have a few more men than this Isagoras?'

'Of course, these are just a few citizens who are accompanying me. Follow me and I'll take you to my supporters.'

Isagoras and his citizens walk off leaving the Spartans to follow, Cleomenes and his fellow Spartans swiftly follow behind. Leonidas's horse is reluctant to walk; he pulls on the horse to encourage it to move, as it huffs in disagreement and begins to walk, unenthusiastically.

After a few minutes of walking, they enter a clearing where Isagoras's supporters wait patiently for their Spartan support. Cleombrotus stops in his tracks as soon as he notices the crowd ahead.

'How many men are here?' He moves his eyes over the crowd of supporters to guess the number.

Before he can guess, Isagoras replies, 'approximately fifteen hundred. This will be enough to expel Cleisthenes and other member of the Alcmaeonidae family.'

'What about the Boule?'

The Boule is a council of five hundred citizens, appointed to run daily and political affairs of the city. Abolishing the council will eradicate any chances of a democratic Athens.

'We'll wipe the lot of them out easily with your support Cleomenes; they will never anticipate our arrival.'

Cleomenes nods his head in agreement. 'What do you think, Spartans?'

Alec and Tiro shrug their shoulders while nodding their heads at the same time. Leonidas and Cleombrotus look concerned.

Leonidas approaches Cleomenes, 'when something seems this straight forward, that's because it generally isn't. Do you trust

Isagoras enough to know he's got a full proof plan? Otherwise, our heads will end up on spikes throughout this bloody city.'

'Look around Leonidas, he looks organised to me.' Cleombrotus turns to Isagoras. 'When do we start, my friend?' Isagoras turns to the crowd of supporters raising his arms in the air. 'We start now!'

The crowds of supporter's cheer and embrace one another as if this symbolises the start of a new beginning, a better Athens.

Unbeknown to them, one of the supports had betrayed Isagoras and has sided with Cleisthenes, telling him about the Spartan intervention and supporters willing to try and expel Cleisthenes, his family and the Boule.

Fortunately, for Cleisthenes this gave him enough time to gather his thoughts, supporters and a plan of counter attack. Portraying Isagoras as a tyrant, Cleisthenes has been able to hugely outnumber Isagoras with pro-democratic Athenian citizens, that were eager to revolt against his plans.

Cleisthenes and his supporters wait deep within the city walls for further instructions. With such huge numbers, Cleisthenes is confident he will be able to run Isagoras and his ally Spartans out of the city.

It had been a long day and the evening draws in on Athens, the cool evening breeze was a relief for the Spartans, cooling their hot skin from the exposure of the day's sun.

Isagoras and the Spartans have spent much of the afternoon going over their plans. Isagoras knows this evening will be the night the Boule will conduct a meeting and he will use this as a distraction to ambush the council, and immediately exile all of them out of the city, before locating and exiling their families and other citizens who side with Cleisthenes.

The Spartans prepare themselves and fill their bellies. Tiro gulps down his wine and wipes the drips from his chin with his forearm. 'If Cleisthenes has any sense or has got wind of us in the city, he should be thinking about leaving before we find him.'

Alec nods his head in agreement, 'What if we have any resistance, strike them down?'

'Yes, absolutely,' replies Cleomenes, as he looks over his sword to check its condition.

'Right then, time to make our move,' says Isagoras, clapping his hands to enthuse everyone to move quicker.

The evening was calm, despite feeling eerily quiet few citizens had any reason to be out within the streets of Athens at this time of night. Athens has thousands of houses and buildings resulting in a complex network of streets, some dimly lit but the majority, in complete darkness.

Isagoras and his supporters split in to four large groups, Cleomenes and Isagoras leading the first group. Leonidas and Cleombrotus leading the second, Tiro the third and Alec the fourth.

The narrow streets create an illusion of their groups being much larger than they appear, as they are forced in some areas to be just three or four men across.

The plan is to surround and block each side of the council building and ambush everyone inside from every angle, overwhelmingly out numbering the members inside. The building was huge surrounded by countless limestone columns, so tall that anyone would think they were built by giants or the Gods themselves. It was gently lit by several fire baskets around the perimeter that elongated the men's shadows the full length of the street.

Three of the four groups are in place. The group led by Cleomenes and Isagoras approach last, making their way slowly towards the main entrance. All will unleash hell on the signal.

One man from each group lights their torch using the fire baskets. Once Cleomenes and Isagoras breach the front entrance the first torch bearer will raise his torch high in the air, followed by the remaining torch bearers indicating to their groups to advance.

Isagoras looks at Cleomenes, to remain silent he only uses his fingers to count, *one, two, three.*

The first group storms the entrance simultaneously as the torch bearer flings his torch up high above his head. Within seconds, all four groups have stormed the building. To their surprise, the building is empty.

Cleomenes pauses abruptly in disbelief, breathing hard from the adrenaline coursing through his veins. 'What's going on here, Isagoras?'

'Shit!' replies Isagoras, still looking around for any sign of why the building is empty.

Suddenly, a lot of commotion can be heard from outside and many of his supporters flee the building to see what is happening.

The streets are flooded with hundreds of Athenian citizens, vastly outnumbering the four groups.

'It's a revolt! They must have known we were coming!' says Leonidas, as he fends off an attacker by kicking the fire basket over, smothering his attacker in hot ambers before plunging his sword in to the citizen's abdomen.

The roars of citizen's could be heard echoing throughout the city streets and it quickly became clear that they are up against the majority of Athens population. The citizens had armed themselves with anything they could get their hands on, some wielding swords, spears and knives, others with rocks and sticks.

Isagoras and the Spartans have managed to meet in a huddle surrounded by angry Athenians demanding they are cut down. They fend off the attackers for as long as they can but there are too many coming from every angle, and more keep appearing from the surrounding streets in waves.

A clearing has presented itself ahead. 'Look, we can fight our way through there!' Alec says, encouraging his comrades to follow.

'Follow the Spartans!' Isagoras shouts at his supporters, waving his arm to encourage them to retreat from the fighting. Many manage their way through before the rest are cut down and beaten, unable to escape the vast numbers appearing from every building and street.

'We need to take high ground,' Demands Cleomenes.

'Up there!' suggests Cleombrotus, pointing up to the limestone hill, towards the Acropolis. 'We can take a short cut through those trees.'

'Follow me!' Isagoras knows the way and leads the Spartans and his followers up the steep climb to the Acropolis.

They eventually reach the top and pause to gather their breath with the three hundred followers that have also reached the top, with some still ascending. Turning to look over the edge of the hill top and observe the chaos in the streets below, a continuous line of orange dots zigzags through the streets as hundreds of citizens with lit torches continue their search for the Spartans and Isagoras.

Before long the revolt begins to make its way up the hillside towards the Acropolis. 'We don't have much time,' says Leonidas, looking around to try and figure a way out of the city.

'Quickly everyone, we will not outrun the masses, let's take shelter in there.' Pointing at the old temple, Isagoras leads the way.

Tiro couldn't help but feel overwhelmed by the sheer size of the structure, its size made him feel completely inferior. The brilliant white limestone structure highlighted with vibrant colours and dozens of brilliantly sculptured statues, with exquisite detail.

'It's no wonder that Athens carries a reputation of wealth and power, if anything, it looks the part.'

'Shut up, Tiro.' Leonidas helps push Tiro up the first step which required a large stride to clear it.

As they enter the old temple, immediately adjacent to the entrance is a thirty-foot statue of Athena, made from solid gold and ivory.

Their eyes widen as they marvel at the sculpture, Alec's jaw drops at the sight of so much gold.

'Of course, why wouldn't there be a huge golden statue in here, it makes complete sense.' Trying to make light of the predicament they are in.

'Isagoras,' shouts one of his supporters from across the old temple, we have someone of interest for you who we captured on our way here.'

'Who is it?'

'It is a member of the Boule, but more importantly a relation of Cleisthenes.'

'That's great. At least we may now have some leeway to negotiate our way out of here.'

It doesn't take long before the Acropolis is rampant with an angry mob and the old temple is completely surrounded, with no safe route of escape.

Leonidas looks over at Cleomenes, 'I hope this relative is worth three hundred lives to Cleisthenes, otherwise we are as good as dead.'

12

Two days have passed, Cleisthenes has intentionally ignored all requests to negotiate with Isagoras. His followers and the Spartans are thirsty, hungry and frustrated. Some of Isagoras's supporters could not stand the waiting around and fled out of the temple in a panic, only to be struck down by the Athenian Mob.

Frustrated, Leonidas steps forward, 'Enough of the soft approach, if they want us to die by the sword or starvation then we have nothing to lose. Send Cleisthenes a message he will respond to.'

'What do you suggest, brother?' replies Cleombrotus.

'We have a hostage who is useless to us if we are going to die anyway, cut his head off and throw it to the mob.'

'No, not yet,' Cleomenes responds, looking deep in thought.

'Think about it, we have been here for two days and the revolt hasn't even attempted to enter the temple and Cleisthenes hasn't said a word.'

Alec scratches his head with an expression of confusion, 'Are you suggesting this is part of his plan, make us fear for our lives in order to better negotiate?'

'Possibly, but he forgets one thing?'

'And, that is?'

'Spartans fear nothing.'

Tiro laughs out loud, 'No, but we sit in here like cowards to avoid being dismantled.'

'Don't you get it?' Cleisthenes wants us to feel fear, to feel he is in control. If he wanted us dead, we would be hanging from a rope by now. This suggests one thing, he needs us,' responds Cleomenes.

Cleisthenes's plan is working, leaving Isagoras and the Spartans to the mercy of the Athenian mob while hungry and frustrated will make it easier for them to agree to his terms.

While the Athenian mob continues to revolt on the Acropolis under Cleisthenes's instruction, he and his noblemen discuss their plans.

'We will leave them in there another night; tomorrow morning, I will state my terms.'

'What if they do not agree?' one of the noblemen asks curiously.

'Then they die, they are not in any position to negotiate otherwise,' – Cleisthenes wears a smug grin on his face - 'I only have one proposal to offer and that is for Isagoras to be exiled or executed, his choice. His supporters, who call themselves Athenian citizens will be left to the mercy of the revolt.'

The noblemen cheer in response to Cleisthenes. 'What about the Spartans?'

'Well, let's just say we can use them to do our dirty work, unless they want to die of course and leave their city to burn to the ground, what's left of it anyway.'

The morning of day three, Isagoras and the Spartans are at their wits end. More of Isagoras's supporters have taken the chance to flee, only to be struck down before reaching the first step of the old temple.

During the previous evening, the Spartans had to fend off some of the Athenian mob who took it upon themselves to try their chances at taken on a Spartan, instantly regretting their decision.

Tiro picked himself up off of the floor where he had been laying, bored and hungry. 'We need to move; it is clear Cleisthenes wants us to die a slow death from starvation.'

'Starvation or boredom,' Alec sarcastically replies.

Suddenly, the noise and commotion outside dulls down. Isagoras looks through a gap in the doorway to observe what is happening.

The crowd parts, 'It is Cleisthenes, he's coming over here.' Isagoras starts to open the doorway.

'Wait,' shouts Cleomenes, followed by a few stray objects clashing against the outside of the door.

Cleisthenes approaches the base of the old temple on horseback; he dismounts and precedes to climb the first few steps.

'Isagoras, Spartans, I have a proposal for you to consider. Please come out, you have my word no harm will come of you.'

'Bollocks,' a voice from inside the temple shouts in disbelief.

'Brother, this is a trap I do not have a good feeling about this,' Leonidas says to Cleomenes, concerned for their safety. 'This is way to get us out and humiliate us in front of his supporting crowd, do not give him the satisfaction.'

Cleomenes pauses momentarily to consider his options, but there are none. 'What other choice do we have Leonidas? If it's a trap, then let's show them how dangerous a hungry and tired Spartan can be.'

Alec and Tiro poise themselves as Isagoras opens the doors. The sunlight was bright and intense on their eyes, squinting to try and focus on what's outside.

Isagoras walks out with one hand partially over his brow to stop the sunlight hurting his eyes. He observes Cleisthenes using a waving gesture to encourage them to come down.

As they begin to ascend the step and get closer to Cleisthenes, he puts his arms out to indicate that he has no intention to draw a weapon.

'I'm not interested in fighting; I need to talk and you need to listen. However, I assure you once I am finished talking, you will only have two options. Do what I say or die, the choice is yours.

Isagoras smirks at Cleisthenes, 'Decisions, decisions,' he mumbles.

Isagoras and the Spartans cautiously watch their backs as they edge closer to Cleisthenes to hear what he has to say.

They need to turn their ears closer to Cleisthenes in order to hear above the roar of the crowd that has stirred around them.

Cleisthenes steps in to Isagoras wearing a smug grin on his face, as he takes great pride in being able to tell him his proposal.

'You have not prevailed Isagoras, you have failed miserably and you should be thankful I have not yet removed your head. You are an over ambitious figure with strong opinions but unfortunately, they do not align with the future of Athens.'

Isagoras raises his eyebrows and rolls his eyes towards Cleomenes.

'Ok so I still have my head attached, where is this conversation going, Cleisthenes?'

'I'm glad you ask Isagoras, because with immediate effect you are to be ostracised.'

'Ostracised?'

'Yes, you are being expelled from the city state of Athens for a minimum of ten years. If you refuse, you die. If you return without permission, you die.'

Isagoras looks shocked as the blood drains from his face, leaving him as white as the limestone he stands on. This was a big blow for Isagoras and his political ambitions; with no other choice besides death, he bows his head in shame, accepting his fate.

'Assuming we are in agreement, Isagoras, my men will now escort you out of my city.'

Isagoras turns to Cleomenes, he doesn't say a word, just a gentle nod of his head as a sign of his appreciation.

'One more thing before you go,' - placing a hand on his shoulder - 'All of your supporters that are still awaiting their fate in the old temple, they will all be executed to set an example that this city will not give in to the likes of you. Their blood will be on your hands.'

The Spartans are equally as shocked, their plan to infiltrate Athens with Isagoras is now ruined. Cleomenes must return to

Sparta with his tail between his legs and explain to the Ephors why the plan he convinced would work, has failed.

'Cleomenes, I have a special task for you and you fellow Spartans.'

Cleomenes folds his arms and lifts his chin, curiously listening. 'And what is this, special task?'

'Invade Aegina.'

Aegina is one of the Saronic Islands of Greece; it is one of Greece's early maritime powers, famous for minting the earliest coins in Greece which are accepted all over the Mediterranean region. Athens and Aegina have become enemies over a feud involving statues of two deities; however, it is more likely that Athens has grown envious of the island's prosperity, further concerned over their trade with Persia.

'You want me to invade Aegina…for you?' Cleomenes was taken aback by such an ambitious proposal.

'Yes.'

'Why?'

'Athens needs to punish Aegina for their act of medism. They have decided to collaborate with the Persians and I will not let that go unnoticed.'

Leonidas kisses his teeth denoting mild disapproval and shaking his head in disbelief, 'You can't be serious, Cleisthenes?'

Cleisthenes laughs hard enough that he has to hold his stomach in with his hand; it was a laugh of confidence, satisfied in knowing the Spartans had no other option.

'I am very serious, Spartan, and if you do not get approval from your Ephors then Athens will bring you Hades himself. I am pretty sure your city is not in the condition to negotiate, hence why you came to Isagoras in the first place. Now I am giving you an opportunity to side with the right person and for a truce between Sparta and Athens.'

Cleomenes turns to his comrades, 'Ok, Cleisthenes, we'll help you invade Aegina. I just need some time.'

'You have seven days, that's enough time to return home and convince your council to round up your warriors. Now leave!'

The Spartans move on through the parting crowd as they are shoved, spat on and heckled off of the Acropolis.

Alec and Tiro turn back towards the temple to see their hostage embrace Cleisthenes, while all of Isagoras's supporters are dragged out and thrown to the ground, some tumbling down the steep temple steps.

'Kill them all, not one of these traitors leaves here alive,' Cleisthenes demands, as he mounts his horse.

They are hugely outnumbered and it takes only a few moments before each and every one of them is engulfed, hacked to pieces and clubbed to death.

Once off of the Acropolis, the Spartans are given back their horses and led out of the city. They ride off in silence as they contemplate the previous few days.

Cleomenes is deep in thought already thinking about how he is going to persuade the council to invade Aegina.

Leonidas thinks of Gorgo and how he is grateful he is still alive and able to see her again. Then at that moment, without any consideration he turns to Cleomenes, 'Gorgo and I are in love!'

Cleomenes stops his horse, 'I know.'

'You do?'

'Gorgo has been sneaking around and I have observed the way you both look at each other, I am not stupid. However, if you are looking for my approval, brother, just because we have been through a small ordeal, you will not have it and you never will. I have plans for Gorgo and they don't involve you.'

Cleombrotus, Tiro and Alec look at one another awkwardly as the tension in the air became thick. Leonidas was furious but didn't know what to say. Cleomenes is the King and Gorgo is his daughter, it was suddenly clear to Leonidas as long as Cleomenes is around he will never be able to be with Gorgo.

Leonidas looked across to Cleombrotus who retuned his gaze, shrugging his shoulders. It was then clear, if Leonidas was to successfully plan on becoming King and Gorgo his Queen, Cleomenes must die.

13

Finally arriving in Sparta, albeit filthy, tired, dehydrated and hungry, Cleomenes must now approach the council of elders at the earliest opportunity.

The others all return back to their quarters and clean themselves up before over filling their bellies, sending them off to sleep. However, Cleomenes cannot rest and he makes his way to the council.

Cleomenes has explained the events to date but has cleverly not let on they were ambushed and captured, avoiding any shame. Instead, Cleomenes has convinced the council Isagoras had already been caught and ostracised before their arrival and instead struck a deal with Cleisthenes that could potentially bring together a truce between Sparta and Athens. Something his Father failed to do.

Cleomenes finishes notifying the council on his recommendations, stating for the truce to happen they must invade Aegina. The council becomes lively in discussion and takes several minutes to calm down.

Demaratus sits slouched in his seat with his arms folded, shaking his head in disagreement. 'Nonsense, what kind of King makes an agreement with a rival state to use our resources to fight their battles, without consulting the council or the Oracle?'

'A King that improvises and prioritise Sparta's needs, what would you suggest, King Demaratus? Please, enlighten the council with your experience and wisdom.'

Demaratus fell silent with embarrassment, unable to provide a better option. He glared at Cleomenes who calmly smirked back.

'I didn't think you had much else to say because you were not there, you conveniently remained here in the comfort of your home.'

Demaratus looked around the council and could see some of the elders nodding in agreement with Cleomenes and lightly sniggering to themselves behind their hands. Demaratus had every intention to get his own back on Cleomenes and would go to great lengths to succeed.

The council approves Cleomenes to cross over to Aegina and supply him with the men he needs. Demaratus storms out furiously, frustrated that he has been ignored and made to feel foolish.

'Now that is settled, I will send a message to Cleisthenes to send his ships. Our men will be ready to set sail in four days,' Cleomenes says, proudly addressing the council.

A few days pass and the Athenian Ships have yet to arrive. The Spartan army is ready as they camp at their port, twenty-seven miles south of Sparta, but the ships never came.

Cleomenes grew increasingly inpatient trying to understand why Cleisthenes would not send his ships.

'Damn those Athenians, they just can't be trusted.'

Cleomenes and his men would camp for the night on the off chance they would arrive late. If the Athenian ships are not at port by sunrise then Cleomenes and his men plan to return back to Sparta.

The next morning, Cleomenes cannot sleep and is awake several hours before sunrise, standing at the port looking out to sea. Eventually, the sun begins to appear and Cleomenes watches it rise quickly as a burst of fiery orange cascades across the sky and over the port, momentarily turning the sea yellow and the surface glisten, as if sprinkled in jewels.

Cleomenes places both hands on his hips and releases a sigh of disappointment. On their journey home, he can't help but think how two consecutive plans have failed and the smug look that will be on the face of Demaratus.

'Demaratus,' Cleomenes thought to himself. *'This can't be a coincidence; it reeks of interference and he must be responsible.'*

Cleomenes was right in his suspicions; little did he know Demaratus had someone intercept the messenger to prevent the message getting to Athens. Cleisthenes is none the wiser and believes Cleomenes has backed out of their deal.

The council of elders hears of the return of Cleomenes and instantly sends for him to address the council with an explanation.

Before the meeting can start, Demaratus wastes no time in sharing his thoughts.

'Well, Cleomenes fails once again to build a truce with Athens, just like his Father and yet nobody would listen to me.'

The council begins to mumble as Demaratus speaks.

'Cleomenes is a liability and cannot be trusted; he has proved this time and again.'

Cleomenes addresses the council, 'I have kept my end of the deal, how was I to know Cleisthenes wouldn't?'

After much deliberation and to the dismay of Demaratus, the council agrees with Cleomenes, this was out of his control.

The council is interrupted; a messenger from Athens has arrived to deliver a message to Cleomenes. It is from Cleisthenes stating his anger at not receiving confirmation regarding their deal, and unless his messenger returns with good news, Sparta will fall.

'I sent a messenger,' Cleomenes says out loud, sounding confused. 'Cleisthenes clearly states he didn't arrive, but there would have been no threat towards him along the way.' Cleomenes ponders momentarily.

He looks up and glares at Demaratus who suddenly begins to look nervous. Cleomenes storms over to Demaratus, without hesitating he punches him square on the chin, sending him crashing to the floor and snapping his head back as it thuds on to the ground, nearly rendering him unconscious.

'You piece of shit, Demaratus. This was all your doing wasn't it? You couldn't help yourself but to interfere You made your views very clear then coincidently, the messenger suddenly disappears.'

Demaratus sits up rubbing his chin and the back of his head that throbs in pain. 'You can't prove that Cleomenes, this is just another one of your wild theories.'

Cleomenes nods, 'Ok, you continue to play it like this and we'll see where you end up.'

'Is that a threat, Cleomenes?'

'No, it's a promise!'

Cleomenes addresses the council one more time. 'It is clear now Cleisthenes did not receive the message,' - He looks down and snarls at an unstable Demaratus, climbing off of the floor - 'I propose we get someone to escort Cleisthenes messenger back, stating that we are ready and we will meet them where originally agreed. No more interruptions!'

'Very well then, the last thing we need is an invasion on our own city,' the council agrees enthusiastically.

It is clear to Cleomenes that Demaratus will never see eye to eye with him and that he will do all it takes to have him banished. Therefore, Cleomenes must counter Demaratus, before it's too late.

That evening, Cleomenes decides to locate a relative and enemy of Demaratus who goes by the name, Leotychidas. Leotychidas was a member of the Eurypontid dynasty and cousin to Demaratus. Cleomenes has come up with a plan to dethrone Demaratus in favour for Leotychidas.

After searching for some time, Cleomenes finally locates Leotychidas. 'You are a hard man to find, Leotychidas,' recognising his voice.

'Yes, when I don't want to be found, Cleomenes,' he replies, with a smile. They both embrace happy to see one another.

'It's been a long time Cleomenes, ruler of Sparta,' he says laughing.

'Shut up, I am here to offer you a proposal that you might be interested in.'

'Go on.'

'It's regarding your cousin.' Cleomenes expects a reaction.

'Are you referring to Demaratus? Fuck off, I am not interested; he's making a mockery of our dynasty in a position that is rightly mine.'

'Yes, and that is why I am here, old friend. It may involve bribing the Oracle and convincing the council, but I believe we can pull it off.' He places his arm around Leotychidas.

Leotychidas partially closes his eyes and glares at Cleomenes. 'Are you suggesting what I think you are?'

Cleomenes gives Leotychidas a firm pat on the back. 'We will reign long together, side by side. Banish Demaratus and finally rule as one.'

Leotychidas cannot believe what he is hearing. 'I need to hear you say it.'

'Ok, I want you to be the next King of the Eurypontid dynasty. Not just the King but the rightful King.'

Leotychidas looks shocked and never thought he would ever be approached for such a task once Demaratus was made King. Leotychidas shakes his head, 'No, the council will never agree to this.'

'I can deal with the council; they have already made it clear that I am the more favourable one. Come on Leotychidas, don't stand there pretending you are thinking about it, it's your birth right.'

Leotychidas momentarily turns away from Cleomenes; he folds his arms and makes a clicking sound with his tongue, as he thinks the proposal through.

'Well, Leotychidas. I haven't got all night, so why don't you think a little faster,' said Cleomenes, impatiently waiting for a response.

Leotychidas turns sharply to face Cleomenes. 'The council mustn't know you've approached me first, otherwise this will look suspicious.'

'Yes, ok, you have my word.'
'In that case…When can I Start?'
Cleomenes returns a huge smile of gratitude and makes on his way.

14

Cleomenes is discussing his plans to expel Demaratus with his brothers, Leonidas and Cleombrotus; they are all in agreement that Demaratus must go in order to have a truce with Athens.

'I have one issue, brother; how do we convince the council this is the right decision?' Cleombrotus nods his head in agreement to Leonidas's question.

'We don't; I will bribe the Oracle to agree with my plan. All I need to do then, is convince the council that the right thing to do is to consult the Oracle.'

'Let's hope the Oracle accepts the bribe then, brother. The council won't dare go against the guidance of the Priestess.'

'I'm counting on it.'

Later that day, Cleomenes has made his way to see the Oracle, to his surprise she was already in a trance like state. The yellow mist engulfs her body swirling around her limbs and over her face, taking in a large lungful through her mouth and exhaling it out of her nose. The Oracle's eyes open wide, the pupils appear black as night. She glares straight at Cleomenes, making him feel uneasy, as if looking through his soul.

'I've been expecting you, King Cleomenes,' she whispers, as her body contorts.

'I can see that.' Cleomenes uses his hand to fan away the yellow mist that mingles around his face and stings his eyes.

He drops a sack filled with a variety of foods, grain, wine, several sheep fleece's and a small bag of gold far exceeding anything she is accustom to. The mist started to clear and the Oracle's breathing began to calm, signaling to Cleomenes to come closer. He reluctantly approaches, wearing a disgruntled look due to the strange smell of the remaining mist that dispersed around him as he walks through it.

He leans in, 'I need you to pronounce in favour of my recommendation to the council, as they will consult with you shortly regarding the birth right of King Demaratus. He has no birth right.'

The Oracle edges closer, stopping close to his lips, so close he could smell her stale breath that hinted at the smell of hallucinogens. The Oracle looks at the bribe Cleomenes has brought and then gently strokes her finger down Cleomenes's lips, indicating her silence and acceptance of the bribe. She doesn't say anything further and flicks her fingers twice towards the doorway. Cleomenes acknowledges her decision with a respectful nod and leaves the temple.

By the time Cleomenes returns, it is early evening and he wastes no time in requesting a meeting with the council. Demaratus is present and looks unsure as to why Cleomenes has requested an unplanned meeting.

'So, Cleomenes, what is it you would like to so desperately bring to our attention that cannot wait until the morning?' one of the elder's asks.

'It's Demaratus; he must be abdicated with immediate effect.'

'What is this here?' Demaratus erupts in to a rage putting his arms out to declare his innocence in any matter.

'Council, it is clear Demaratus is not fit to be King. He has no interest in a truce with Athens or playing a part in negotiations, he sabotage's our plans to invade Aegina which he didn't deny when I pressed him on the matter, an invasion authorised by you on an island that supports the Persians. If I didn't know any better, I would say he is colluding with the Persians.'

'I have never heard so much...' Cleomenes doesn't allow Demaratus to speak, cutting him off part way through his sentence.

'This all makes sense now; it is no secret there is doubt surrounding his birth right as King, his actions prove this.'

'I've never heard such rubbish.' Demaratus is shaking with anger, feeling blindsided and betrayed.

'The problem we have here council is that he cannot prove otherwise, nor can we. However, even the tiniest of doubt should be enough.'

'You've made your point, Cleomenes,' one of the elder's says. 'There is only one way to clarify this matter and that is to visit the Delphic Oracle.'

'What a great idea,' Cleomenes confirms.

The meeting abruptly adjourns. 'We will consult with the Oracle and return back here at first light tomorrow morning,' Lycurgus declares. 'Demaratus, if you are rightfully King then you have Sparta's best interests. If you have nothing to hide, the Oracle will tell us either way.'

The following morning the council reconvenes at the Gerousia. 'Demaratus, stand before the council,' Lycurgus bellows. It had been a long and restless night for Demaratus, the anxiety of not knowing his fate as King lay in the balance. He remained calm but inside he was accumulating so much hate towards Cleomenes he could feel the burning sensation deep within his belly. As the council spoke, he gritted his teeth in frustration.

'Demaratus, with immediate effect the council declare your abdication as King of the Eurypontid dynasty. The doubt of your birth right as King was finally confirmed by the Oracle, you are not the legitimate son of your so-called Father, King Ariston, but of Agetus, something I fear we should have addressed much sooner. You have brought shame on the Eurypontid dynasty. Therefore, you will leave Sparta immediately; once you have left, your house will be burnt to the ground.'

For the first time Demaratus felt completely powerless, the council would never listen to an appeal. Whatever the Oracle states is what must be followed.

Cleomenes stands and addresses the council, feeling elated with the council's decision. 'I believe the rightful King of the Eurypontid dynasty is Leotychidas and that he will be notified accordingly?'

'Yes, you are correct Cleomenes; Leotychidas is being notified as we speak.'

'Very well, Sir,' Cleomenes replies, struggling to contain himself with excitement.

As Demaratus is being escorted away and removed from the city, Cleomenes uses the opportunity to suggest another attempt at invading Aegina.

'With Leotychidas as the new Eurypontid King I feel it is the ideal opportunity to invade Aegina and finally complete this truce with Athens. This can only benefit Sparta.' Cleomenes passionately clenches his first on to his chest to emphasise his enthusiasm.

'Very well, if there is a time when we need a truce then it's now, two Kings replaced from each dynasty could make Sparta look unorganised, weak and unable to control our own leadership. A truce with Athens will seal our place as a landmark of authority within these lands.'

Cleomenes nods his head, 'Couldn't agree with you more.'

Later that day, Leotychidas stood in the Gerousia where he was officially confirmed as King of the Eurypontid Dynasty and his first priority was to support Cleomenes on his campaign to invade Aegina. The importance of this task does not go unnoticed; there was no room for error this time around. With Demaratus out of the way Cleomenes would no longer have any excuse for failure, it was his time to shine and prove his allegiance to Sparta and convince Athens of a long-awaited truce.

Cleisthenes has agreed to supply the ships with crew members to aid their journey and has provided Cleomenes with strict instructions to detain the ten leading citizens that are responsible, depositing them to Athens where they will be held hostage. Unlike the first attempt, the Kings will march their men to Athens before crossing over to Aegina.

Cleomenes later approaches Alec and Tiro, 'Listen up Spartans; you are to accompany Leotychidas and myself to

Aegina where we will invade the island and bring back hostages to deposit to Athens.'

'Yes, my King, but why are you telling us individually?' replies Alec.

'Because I need you both to lead our soldiers under my command and according to my brothers Leonidas and Cleombrotus, you two are the best. We leave in two days.'

Cleomenes leaves to prepare for his departure and inform Leonidas and Cleombrotus to hold firm in Sparta while he is away.

Tiro looks at Alec and notices a change in his colour, 'What's wrong with you? You're turning green!' Tiro begins to laugh uncontrollably.

'Shut your mouth, Tiro. The thought of being at sea makes me want to heave. These aren't sea fairing legs; they are meant to remain firm on land,' Alec replies, irritably.

'It's going to be a long trip for you then boy, you best start preparing yourself.' Tiro unsympathetic to Alec's predicament.

Tiro believes the trip will be an easy victory; he has spent little time at sea but is not too concerned about the journey. The Saronic Gulf is known for its calm waters as it is one of the main trading routes. Therefore, it should be a reasonably calm crossing.

What Cleomenes would fail to acknowledge was the readiness of the Aeginetans. In Aegina they were preparing for battle after word travelled of the first failed attempt. They patiently wait on standby, anticipating the second attempt of invasion.

The Kings and their crew were midway through their journey, the sea wasn't being kind to them as the Saronic Gulf continued to batter the ships in to near submission, claiming them hers.

Alec tried to hide his anxiety holding on so tightly to the side of the ship his knuckles turning white, as he vomits over the side, only for the waves to wash it back over in to the ship.

'Fuck the Gods,' Alec mumbled to himself, wiping the sick off of his chin with his forearm.

'You love it!' shouted Tiro from across the deck, who was entertained by Alec's suffering, despite feeling sick himself he failed to show it. 'We are nearly there my friend.' Feeling guilty and wanting to provide some encouragement.

Despite the high coastal winds, the sky was clear and the visibility was good, Aegina was now becoming visible each time the ship rode the top of waves, quickly disappearing as the ships sailed back down them.

A few miles off of the shore and the sea became significantly calmer, much to Alec's relief. The Athenian ships began to coordinate their arrival at the capitals port on the north-west coast, it was reported that the ten leaders requested by Cleisthenes would be there. As they approach, Tiro notices a temple overlooking the port to the north, he notices a small group of people running to its location and one man signaling on the cliff edge towards the port.

'What is that place?' Tiro asks Cleomenes, pointing towards the temple.

'That's the temple of Apollo.'

'I see plenty of activity up there,' said Tiro, walking further up the deck to get a closer look.

Cleomenes and Leotychidas were both unaware that their arrival was expected; the locals were now in hiding after receiving the signal from the hilltop of their arrival and were waiting patiently for the Spartans to disembark.

However, Cleomenes had good instincts in these situations and could sense something was not quite right, despite thinking they didn't know of his arrival he was still expecting some commotion, not a deserted town that is usually busy with traders. Cleomenes and Leotychidas ordered their men off of the ships while Alec and Tiro ordered their formation on land.

The Spartans walked further inland, hesitant to split up, they were suddenly charged at by an orchestrated revolt from every direction, in their masses. There was no formation in their attack and it was very much a free for all, something the Spartans could comfortably deal with.

'Spartans, Shields!' Cleomenes and Leotychidas shout simultaneously. Every Spartan raises their shield.

Tiro notices a gap in their link, 'Tighten your phalanx.'

Not one solider is more important than the other, the Spartans lock closely together forming one large single unit in a mass coordinated maneuver. Each shield was three feet in diameter; suddenly the Aeginetans were facing a sheer wall of bronze. This was an intimidating site to behold and it was a common mistake to think a mass of bodies charging the wall of shields would break the Spartan phalanx.

The Spartans stand firm as the Aeginetans bounce off their shields, followed by a barrage of spears accurately thrusting through the smallest of gaps.

The Spartans advance in unison, taking down each new wave of attackers one by one.

'This is just too easy,' Alec shouts with a smile on his face, enjoying what they have long trained for.

It takes a matter of moments before the streets fall silent once again; the port is full of bodies stretching from one end of the port through to the other. Some of the bodies that fell in to the sea roll on and off of the beach with the tide, turning the water and sand red. Despite their enthusiasm and readiness, the Aeginetans didn't stand a chance.

Leotychidas approaches Cleomenes, 'Any ideas where the ten leaders could be?'

'I wouldn't mind betting they are in hiding, up there,' - Cleomenes points up the hill towards the temple of Apollo - 'I will send a small group of Spartans up there to retrieve them while we wait down here and clear the area thoroughly, and then we can be on our way.'

Alec and Tiro are instructed to take five men each to the temple of Apollo and bring the ten leaders back to their ships before darkness, killing anyone that stands in their way.

Tiro and his men lead the way and Alec's group follow suit. At first, the climb is steep with narrow footpaths along the cliffs edge. The Spartans can only pass by moving in to single file, their shields wide enough to overhang the cliff edge.

A few loose stones fall from above Tiro's group of men catching Alec's attention, as he looks up, he sees a line of men with huge boulders lifted above their head.

'Tiro look out, above your head,' Alec shouts, feeling exposed and vulnerable on the cliff edge.

Before Tiro can react, he is narrowly missed by a boulder as it is thrown from above, smashing in to the Spartan directly behind him, spraying a mist of blood over Tiro. The Spartan is immediately thrown from the cliff as his body smashes in to the jagged rocks below. Within seconds his body is washed away by the tide.

Another Spartan is struck on the shoulder, as he falls the next Spartan in line attempts to grab his arm but he too is struck by a boulder, sending them both falling to their death.

Alec shouts towards Tiro's direction, 'Use your shields.' They all raise their shields above their heads, but even with protection the boulders are hard to deflect due to their size. The Spartans hurry along the footpath and the bombardment of rocks comes to a halt as they enter open space.

'Fuck,' Tiro says in frustration, not liking that he was caught off guard.

Alec approaches Tiro, 'Are you injured brother?' Observing Tiro's face covered in blood.

'I'm fine, the blood isn't mine, belongs to that poor bastard down there,' Tiro replies, peering over the cliff edge.

Alec looks over Tiro's shoulder towards the temple of Apollo; they are being watched by someone, possibly someone as a look out. The individual knows he has been seen and in a blind panic turns to run knowing he stands an unlikely chance against a Spartan. Alec drops his shield and pushes Tiro to one side to make chase.

Alec is very quick on his feet and he makes up the ground quickly. When he is a few feet away from the individual he pulls out both of his blades without losing any speed. Alec uses an old fallen column to his advantage to push off of with his leg, catapulting himself in to the air landing both blades in to the man's shoulder blades.

They both crash to the floor as Alec neatly rolls forward and back on to his feet. Tiro and the remaining Spartans eventually catch up. When they arrive, Alec is removing the blades that he intentionally prevented from going too deep, he wants to keep the man alive in order to ask questions.

Tiro rolls the man on to his back and punches him in the face, breaking his nose. Alec puts the knife to his throat, 'Where are the ten leaders? We will let you live if you tell us where they are hiding.'

The man looks in the direction of Apollo's temple. 'Good man' - Tiro punches him again - 'are there any surprises or more men in hiding, waiting to kill us?'

'No, they are on their own in the temple,' the man says, scared for his life.

Tiro gives Alec a nod as an indication to get rid of him. Alec doesn't waste a second and slits the man's throat.

The day is closing in, Tiro, Alec and the remaining Spartans sprint over to the temple before any of the leaders have the chance to escape. It was a large temple consisting of thirty-four columns with a grand entrance.

Tiro approaches the temple first, 'Great, another temple. It doesn't feel too long ago we were stuck in one of these.'

'How our fortunes have changed, Tiro, the Gods favour us.'

The Spartans burst through the temple's entrance where the ten leaders cower at one end. They grab them roughly and throw them on to the ground outside of the temple and repeatedly kick them in to submission.

Tiro grabs one of them by the hair, 'Try any tricks, running or anything else to avoid your capture, you die' - Tiro headbutt's the leader who lets out a loud whimper - 'do you all understand?'

All ten nod in agreement as they get back on their feet. Alec usher's them back towards the narrow pathway. As they descend their ships and the Spartans come in to view, the ten leaders stop in their tracks as they notice the chaos and bloodshed that has occurred below.

'Who said you could stop? You need to keep moving.' Tiro kicks one of them in the back that sends him forward in to the rest of the line, losing their footing as they struggle to keep on the pathway and stop themselves from having the same fate as the Spartans, moments earlier.

As they reach the bottom and walk back to port they are greeted by their fellow Spartans.

'Alec, Tiro, get these men on the ship. We will stay here tonight and sail back to Athens at first light.'

'Yes, King Leotychidas, as you wish.'

The fleet finally arrives back in Athens the following afternoon where they are greeted by Cleisthenes. Cleomenes disembarks and approaches him, 'We have the ten leaders you requested. What do you intend to do with them?'

Cleisthenes places a hand on his shoulder, 'Great work Cleomenes, they will be held as hostages for now. I will eventually use them as bribes for negotiations.'

'If I had it my way, I'd execute the lot like you did with Isagoras's men. Catching these ten for you cost me three Spartans.'

Cleomenes smiles, 'I thought you Spartans were always ready to die?'

'Yes, they died in battle but I'd rather it was for a greater cause.'

'Oh, Cleomenes that's not true,' Cleisthenes says with a sigh. 'What greater cause than a truce with Athens?' Cleisthenes puts his hand out as a gesture to confirm their deal. Cleomenes embraces his arm with a firm grip.

'You have your truce, Cleomenes, as promised.'

Tiro and Alec disembark the ships ushering the ten hostages along the water front, handing them over the Cleisthenes's men.

'You have a long march home, Cleomenes. Rest your men here tonight as my guests. Fill your bellies and drink our wine. Hell, sleep with our women, I insist.'

Cleomenes gives him a nod in acknowledgment, 'Very well, we'll leave tomorrow. However, I am only interested in one woman here, the wife of Isagoras.'

Cleisthenes laughs followed by a cough to clear his throat, 'I did hear rumours that you both became well acquainted on your previous trips to Athens. She remains in Athens. I have no qualms with her.'

'I am pleased to hear it.' Cleomenes walks away, catching Tiro ease dropping on their conversation. 'Is there a problem, Tiro?'

'No problem, my King. I am looking forward to our open invitation to Athens women tonight.'

'Don't get too comfortable, Tiro; you can never truly trust these bastards.'

That evening, Cleomenes made his way to see Isagoras's wife to continue their affair, she was surprised to see him as she was not aware, he was in the city. She was also pleased to have some company now Isagoras has been forced out of Athens. She wasted no time in undressing Cleomenes and giving him what he wanted.

Later that evening, Cleomenes was discussing with her the pressures of being a new Spartan King, the trials and tribulations.

'No wonder Demaratus sided with Persia,' she said rolling over to one side, her back facing Cleomenes.

Cleomenes looked confused, 'What did you say? How do you know that?'

'I overheard a couple of Hoplites talking about it yesterday; I guess gossip like that travels quickly through these lands.'

He pulls her back towards him so he can see her face, 'What exactly did you hear? I have obviously been too occupied to hear such gossip.'

'It's not really gossip Cleomenes, it is true. When Demaratus was driven from Sparta, he sought refuge in Persia. Apparently, he has been granted the city of Pergamum and surrounding areas in the northwest.

Cleomenes sat up in disbelief, 'I was right, he was a treacherous bastard after all.' He spits on the floor as a sign of hatred towards him.

Isagoras's wife puts her arm around him encouraging him to lie back down. Instead, he stands up and puts his garments back on.

'Sorry, I must get ready to leave for Sparta before daylight. I hope we can see each other sooner rather than later.' Cleomenes kisses her on the forehead and leaves.

Daylight breaks, Cleomenes and Leotychidas are outside the living quarters where their men are staying as quests. They are all asleep, partially clothed and draped in naked women, at least three to each Spartan. As they enter, Cleomenes uses his leg to roll a woman out of his way then kicks a plate of half-eaten food across the room to get their attention.

'Wake up, assholes.'

Some of the Spartans leap to their feet while the women remain asleep; some are stirring but most are too hung over to wake fully.

'Get yourselves outside.' Leotychidas gives one of the Spartans a kick as he walks out.

'Now, move faster, it's time to get back to Sparta!' Cleomenes shouts.

15

Many seasons have been and gone since the invasion of Aegina and Sparta has made a full recovery under the leadership of King Cleomenes and Leotychidas. The truce with Athens has held up. However, Persia is still creating waves that may create issues for Sparta.

Cleomenes has shown peculiar behaviour in recent months, often talking to himself and smacking his head when he doesn't agree with his own thoughts.

Leonidas has put his duties first before his own desire to lead. However, his time has not been wasted as he rigorously learns the political ways of the land and what the people of Sparta need, including the council. Leonidas spends each day ever increasing his knowledge and chances of becoming the leader he believes Sparta needs, for longevity.

Gorgo and Leonidas spend some alone time together as they walk on the outskirts of Sparta. They are now more open about their relationship since Leonidas informed Cleomenes, but Cleomenes still doesn't approve of their relationship. So, whenever they meet, they do so in private to prevent rubbing Cleomenes the wrong way. Leonidas has already witnessed his capabilities to exile a serving King and for him to suffer the same fate would tear him away from Gorgo.

They both decide to walk towards the Eurotus River, one of Leonidas's favourite locations. They approach the river bank and the water is calm with the sun dazzling and dancing off of its surface. Leonidas closes his eyes to embrace the warmth on his face and to listen to the hypnotic sound of the water cascading over the rocks; a light breeze gently blows a mist of water cooling off his face from the sun.

Gorgo nudges him, 'Look over their Leonidas, is that a body?'

The sun is intense making it hard to see from a distance, so they both walk along the riverbank to get a closer look.

As they approach it appears to be a man partially face down in the shallows of the river. He appears dirty and battered displaying many cuts and bruises.

'It's a Spartan Gorgo.' Leonidas steps in to the river and rolls the body over to see his face. 'Shit, brother, is that you?'

Gorgo frowns in confusion, 'Brother?'

'It's Dorieus, Gorgo. I'll take his arms and you grab his feet.'

Leonidas places Dorieus on the edge of the river bank; he gives him a shake while Gorgo soaks some water up in her tunic to dab on Dorieus's forehead that was exposed and burnt by the sun.

'What is he doing here, Leonidas? Do you think he is dead?'

Leonidas puts his hand on Dorieus's chest, 'I can feel his chest moving, he is alive.'

Moments later, Dorieus starts to groan, choking and coughing up the river water. Leonidas rolls him over on to his side, Dorieus partially opens his eyes.

'Brother, Leonidas, is that really you? he mumbles to himself, spitting out the remaining river water gurgling in the back of his throat.

'Yes, it is me. What the hell are you doing back here? You've got some balls coming back.'

It was unknown how long Dorieus has been travelling or how long he's been in the river, his wounds were partly healed and he looked much older and tired looking.

Dorieus reaches his arm over Leonidas's shoulders, 'Help me to my feet, Leonidas.'

Gorgo steps around to the opposite side of Leonidas and puts Dorieus's other arm over her shoulders. They take him back to their home to clean him up and offer him food and wine. It's not long before Dorieus slowly regains his strength.

Dorieus looks around Leonidas's home and notices several of Gorgo's belongings, 'Are you two . . . Is she . . .?'

'Sort of Dorieus, Cleomenes does not approve so Gorgo does not live here permanently, but things will change soon enough.'

'So, Dorieus, are you going to explain to me why you have returned? The council was pissed when you didn't consult the Delphic Oracle.

'I established and settled a colony at Cinyps. However, it was recently attacked by a tribe called Macae, allies of the Carthaginians' - looking down at the floor in shame - 'I had no choice but to return, I had nowhere else to go.'

Leonidas shakes his head, 'Sounds like you've had a rough time, brother? Let me take you to see Cleomenes and see what we can do for you.'

'No way, I do not want to see Cleomenes. He does not need to know I am here; he already thinks of me as a failure. I would like to speak with the council as I have a new proposal that still keeps me out of Sparta and if I am not mistaken, they would prefer I was out of their way.'

Cleombrotus approaches the house to speak with Leonidas and notices Dorieus through the window. *'Why would he be back here?'* he thought to himself. *'Perhaps he is here to challenge the throne, again; this would ruin all our work to date. I must notify Cleomenes immediately.'*

Cleombrotus finds Cleomenes and notifies him of Dorieus's return to Sparta. Without hesitation Cleomenes storms off in anger to Leonidas's home.

'Where is he, Leonidas? I know he is here.'

'Calm down, Cleomenes, how do you know of this?'

'Cleombrotus has seen him; you should have told me he was here, brother. Can I not trust you?'

'He hasn't been back more than half a day, Gorgo and I found him in the river beaten and exhausted. His colony failed miserably as it fell to a local tribe.'

Cleomenes paces around in frustration, 'Gorgo you say? Keeping more secrets from me, is she?'

Leonidas confronts Cleomenes with confidence, 'You need to calm down, brother. You are acting very erratic.'

'If he thinks he can stroll back in to Sparta and take my rightful place as King, he is in for a shock.'

'I do not believe he is here to take your place as King, he has another proposal for the council but he needs support and funding, that's where he is now.'

Cleomenes grunts at Leonidas and leaves, making his way to the Gerousia.

By the time Cleomenes reaches the Gerousia Dorieus has already approached the council and requested further resources to establish a new colony.

Cleomenes storms in to the building, red faced and angry displaying unpredictable and erratic levels of behaviour.

'I want Dorieus executed; he is reckless and abandoned his duties to Sparta, not to mention he disobeyed your instructions.'

Lycurgus demands order in the council, 'What the hell is this? The only reckless person I see before me is you, Cleomenes.'

Cleomenes calms himself down realising he is making a fool of himself, smacking his head in frustration. Lycurgus and the elders look at one another with a look of concern over his mental state.

Dorieus turns to Lycurgus, 'I think my brother has concerns I am interested in nothing but revenge over him being King. I assure you I have moved on and have no intention of such ambitions.'

Lycurgus takes a deep breath, 'Cleomenes, there will be no execution, his biggest crime is only that of not visiting the Oracle, something he has paid heavily for, he has lost everything, the Gods have already delivered his punishment.'

All the council elders murmur in agreement and Lycurgus continues to speak.

'He still remains a Spartan and descendant of the great King Anaxandridas and is therefore entitled to make requests to the state of Sparta.'

The elders continue to murmur in agreement with Lycurgus, while Cleomenes throws his arms in the air, in frustration.

'Therefore, I would propose that we provide the resources Dorieus needs to establish a new colony on two conditions.'

Dorieus is intrigued, 'What are the conditions?'

'That you establish your colony at Eryx, Sicily. The land rightfully belongs to the Heracleidae, from whom your family claims decent.'

Dorieus nods in agreement, 'The second condition?'

'You will not receive any support until you consult with the Delphic Oracle.'

Dorieus agrees, enthusiastically. Now more cautious of the consequences of not doing this the first time. He leaves the Gerousia and immediately starts his journey to see the Oracle.

The evening is cool and the sky is clear, Leonidas and Gorgo stand on the balcony observing the billions of stars and the moon that's so bright it lights up their courtyard, casting huge shadows of the surrounding columns. A long shadow of a man stretches across the courtyard catching their attention.

'Identify yourself' - Leonidas makes his way to the courtyard - 'Dorieus is that you?'

Dorieus has come directly from Delphi. 'I have been granted permission from the Oracle and the council has confirmed the resources I need will be ready for me at first light.'

Leonidas doesn't say anything. He nods and offers his arm for embrace. Firmly holding one another's forearms there is a moment of mutual respect.

Leonidas senses this will be the last time he will see Dorieus. 'Good luck this time, brother.'

Dorieus smiles and acknowledges the well wishes with a firm nod in return. 'Goodbye Leonidas, my brother.'

16

Cleomenes is requested to return to the Gerousia the following morning. Cleomenes questions their request and begins to feel anxious. Both Leonidas and Cleombrotus are present.

Lycurgus approaches the platform to address the council, 'Council, now the Dorieus situation has been resolved, today we are to discuss the future of the Agiad dynasty regarding a rightful heir to inherit their destiny as King. As we know this must be of the same bloodline as King Cleomenes.'

Cleomenes mumbles to himself, he appears pale and tired as though the pressure of being King has worn him down, or perhaps he is being punished by the Gods. Either way, he is beginning to show signs of unsound mind.

Lycurgus continues, 'Cleomenes, it is about time you started thinking about producing an heir, a son who you can mentor in readiness for his place as King. We have several women perfectly capable of gifting you a son.'

Cleomenes shakes his head and remains silent.

'You're shaking your head because you disagree?'

Despite not realising it at first, it suddenly dawned on Cleomenes that he is in love with Cora, wife of Isagoras and he cannot imagine producing an heir to the throne with anyone else.

'No, I have chosen the woman I want to carry my child,' he said in response.

This came as a surprise to the council as they did not believe this was something Cleomenes had already considered.

'Silence please.' Lycurgus raises his hands to the council to reduce the chatter among the elders. 'Forgive me, I apologise King Cleomenes, you have not mentioned this woman before, please grace the council with her name.'

'Cora, of Athens, wife of the abdicated Aristocrat, Isagoras.'

Leonidas and Cleombrotus could not believe what they were hearing. Cleomenes was putting himself at risk by announcing his affair.

The council became chaotic and Lycurgus was struggling to contain the elders from shouting their opinions out. 'Everyone please be silent,' demands Lycurgus.

The shouting continues but nothing other than the occasional insult can be heard. Cleomenes places his hands over his ears to block the noise, tightly closing his eyes. The council falls silent in dismay that the King is acting in this strange way.

Noticing the silence, Cleomenes opens his eyes and drops his hands from his ears.

'Something wrong, Cleomenes?'

'No, nothing is wrong.'

'Ok then, shall we continue?'

Cleomenes gives Lycurgus a nod of approval.

Lycurgus addresses the council, 'As you can tell Cleomenes, the council doesn't think highly of your choice of woman. There is good reason for this Cleomenes' - placing his hand on his hips - 'Can you honestly stand there before the council and seriously expect us to agree to your choice?'

'What's so hard to accept? You want me to produce an heir, that's who I want to produce it with.'

The shock on Lycurgus's face is blatant. 'So, you are saying Cora, an Athenian who is still married to Isagoras, the man you were helping before supporting his enemy, Cleisthenes?'

'Yes,' he replies sheepishly.

'And how do you think Isagoras will react to that, knowing his so-called ally is not only now supporting his enemy but is having an affair with his wife?' Lycurgus sniggers to himself while the council erupts in laughter. Lycurgus continues, 'This will not be approved, Isagoras can create too many problems for Sparta and we are not prepared to go to war for her.

Upon hearing of their disapproval, Cleomenes storms out of the Gerousia.

'The man must be going mad,' suggests Lycurgus to the council.

Leonidas and Cleombrotus meet in private to discuss the previous events at the Gerousia; both are surprised at the speed of decline of Cleomenes's mind.

'Well, that escalated quickly,' Leonidas says, shaking his head in disbelief. 'What was he thinking?'

'I don't even think he knows the answer to that, but it is definitely something we can play to our advantage.'

'I couldn't agree more.'

'I sense your time is near, Leonidas, I can feel it. The moment the council have their doubts, anyone's time as King is limited.'

'Yes, and with Dorieus now out of the way it is likely our plan will finally come together, after all this time.'

'You'll make a great King, you are what Sparta needs and I have never contested that, we just needed to find the path that leads you there. I have no remorse over our actions, we are obliged to put the needs of Sparta before anything or anyone and that is what we have done. For the greater good of this state.'

'Thank you, brother, but we are not there yet' - embracing his brother firmly - 'I need to find Gorgo and tell her what's happened at the Gerousia.'

Leonidas locates Gorgo at the stables attending her horse; she is pleased to see Leonidas but can see a look of concern on his face.

'Is everything ok, Leonidas?'

'Your Father has been asked to produce an heir by the council but he was acting very strange. He declared he would only consider producing an heir with Cora, wife of Isagoras.'

'Cora, she's nothing but an Athenian whore who married in to wealth.'

'Truer words have never been spoken. Fortunately, the council didn't approve, but I don't think that'll stop Cleomenes doing what he wants.'

'What do you mean?'

'If Isagoras finds out his intentions, it will potentially have devastating consequences for Sparta.'

'I agree, Isagoras is a powerful man.'

'These days seem to be complicated times,' says Leonidas scratching his beard.

Gorgo smiles and embraces him, 'Not that complicated, for Sparta to flourish, you need to be King.'

'You think so, do you?'

'I know so; at least you can produce an heir.'

'What do you mean? he replies, feeling confused.

'I am' – she flicked her hair over her shoulder and looked in to Leonidas's eyes – 'with child, your child.'

Leonidas had no words to express his emotions; all he knew was it reinforced everything that he stood for and fed his passion for wanting to improve Sparta.

'Leonidas, you know this doesn't change anything. My Father will never let us be together, he needs to be abdicated or killed.'

Leonidas nods his head in agreement, 'I understand what needs to be done, it's clearer now.'

Meanwhile, unbeknown to Leonidas, Lycurgus and the elders have been to see the Oracle regarding their doubts over Cleomenes's state of mind. They are rapidly losing confidence in him and his ability to lead Sparta, and produce an heir.

Lycurgus steps forward to pay his respects to the Oracle.

'I am searching for guidance regarding King Cleomenes, he has planted doubt in our minds over his ability to lead and produce an heir.'

The Oracle contorts and fidgets embracing her visions, 'The one you question not only bribes your Gods, but he is unstable in mind.'

Lycurgus looks around to his council members who are listening intensely.

The Oracle continues, 'For Sparta to survive, the lion must rule over his kingdom, for her future is in his hands.' The Oracle falls silent and walks back in to her chambers.

'Leonidas,' whispers Lycurgus.

Lycurgus does not hesitate and immediately sends a request for Leonidas to meet them back at the Gerousia.

Upon their arrival Lycurgus encourages the council to start as soon as possible.

Leonidas stands to address the council, 'I need to inform the council regarding Cleomenes.'

'Save it, we have called you here for good reason. We have been to the Oracle after having doubts of Cleomenes's state of mind.'

'Ok,' he replies, curious to know what's happening.

'An unsound mind is the least of Cleomenes's worries at the moment; he has committed a serious crime.'

Leonidas remains confused, 'I don't understand, you said he's committed a crime?'

'Yes, he has bribed the Gods for his benefit, not Sparta's. To commit a crime against Sparta he must pay the ultimate price.'

'A level even low by his standards,' replies Leonidas.

Lycurgus approaches Leonidas, 'You do know what this means, don't you?

'Yes, I believe so.'

'We have called you here to be provisionally instated as acting King of the Agiad dynasty, until you decide what you want to do with Cleomenes.'

'I live to serve Sparta; whatever it is she requires.'

'Glad to hear it, so what will it be?'

Leonidas takes a few moments to himself to absorb the scale of what was happening, his first decision as acting King is based on the life of his brother. He then thinks of Gorgo and his unborn child, now the real incentive to wanting a better Sparta.

Lycurgus grows impatient for a response. 'Forgive me Leonidas, what would you like to suggest for the crime he has committed?'

Leonidas pulls back his shoulders and stands tall in front of the council.

'Place him in fetters.'

The council agrees to send Spartan soldiers to Cleomenes's home for his arrest.

'I want my brother Cleombrotus there, at his arrest.'

'As you wish,' replies Lycurgus wearing a smile.

Cleomenes is resting within his home when he can suddenly hear the footsteps of marching soldiers. It takes him a matter of seconds before realising what was about to happen. Deep down, he knew this is how things would play out.

He thought to himself, *'How the tides have turned.'* Referring to Dorieus and how he must have felt.

Cleombrotus and the Spartans march towards his home, stopping immediately adjacent to the entrance. Cleombrotus takes two strides forward.

'Cleomenes, you have committed bribery against the Gods and our glorious city Sparta. For this you will be placed in fetters.'

'Bitch,' he thought to himself, referring to the Oracle. He steps outside and the Spartans immediately place him in chains.

'I will not resist your arrest, brother. Is it really necessary to march your King through the city in chains?'

Cleombrotus chuckles to himself, 'The thing is brother' – he says sarcastically – 'you are no longer King.'

'Leonidas, is King?'

Cleombrotus doesn't respond.

Cleomenes bows his head in shame and begins to walk, the chains restricting the length of his natural stride.

It doesn't take long before the citizens start gossiping with wild rumours, some even claiming that Cleomenes killed King Anaxandridas.

Cleomenes is put in to a prison cell that barely has enough room for him to stand in. Cleombrotus pauses momentarily to observe him. However, he remains standing facing the wall where he remains for several hours.

The cell was dark, bleak and small; the smell was unpleasant, created by previous prisoner's defecating because there was nowhere else to go, or they did so out of protest of their incarceration and used it to throw at the guards.

Cleomenes eventually sits down on the floor as a rat walks over his foot, looking for old meal scraps. He contemplates his fate and what options might be presented to him by the council. He knows deep in his heart, if he can't be a Spartan and perform his birth right as King, his life is not worth living.

The little light Cleomenes has entering in to his cell is suddenly blocked out by a figure of a person. He is unable to identify them as the individual is wearing a long-hooded cloak.

'Looks like you've ran in to some trouble,' the cloaked person says quietly.

Cleomenes stands up and edges closer, squinting his eyes tightly as the light silhouettes the figure. 'I recognise that voice. How did you get in here, where are the guards?' – Cleomenes is close enough where the person is able to grab his arm – 'What are you doing here?'

Cleombrotus reports back to Leonidas and the elders at the Gerousia, where they await confirmation of the arrest.

'He is now in chains, as requested,' reports Cleombrotus.

'Did he create any fuss?' asks Lycurgus.

'No, quite the opposite, he was placed in chains and marched to his cell without saying a word.'

'That's because he knows he is guilty.'

Leonidas stands, 'We have matters to discuss here first, then I would like to see him.'

A short time later, the council has finished. Leonidas makes his way to see Cleomenes accompanied by Cleombrotus. A few moments later, Lycurgus catches up with them.

'I'm glad I caught you both before you got there,' – Lycurgus pauses momentarily to catch his breath – 'I have just received a message that something has happened to Cleomenes, doesn't sound good.'

The three of them arrive at the prison cell that is surrounded by Spartan guards.

'What's happening here?' asks Leonidas, pushing his way through the commotion.

The guard's part to clear a path for Leonidas, followed by Cleombrotus and Lycurgus.

Cleomenes is lying on his back in a large pool of blood, his eyes wide open. He is dead.

'Look at his wrist,' Cleombrotus says, pointing to one of them that appears to be slit so deep he would have bled out in a matter of minutes.

Lycurgus reluctantly looks inside, 'Self-mutilation, why would he do that?'

Leonidas orders the corpse to be carried out of the cell, there is no sign of foul play but he does notice something strange. There is no knife blade or other sharp object.

'What did he do it with?'

Lycurgus turns to the guards, 'What did you see or hear?'

'We saw and heard nothing; nobody has been here at all. In fact, you are the first to arrive.'

Leonidas could sense something wasn't right but he had no way to tell if the guards were lying.

'How could he slit his wrist without a blade, did you check if he had a blade on him before you arrested him?'

'No, but he had no idea we were coming. He wouldn't have had time without me noticing,' – he leans on the prison wall and watches the body being removed – 'even if he did, where is it?'

Leonidas remains very suspicious; the cut was far too clean to have been done with anything other than a blade. This raised new concerns for Leonidas. He was potentially looking at having Cleomenes killed but had not confirmed this for definite.

It is clear someone wanted him dead sooner than he did and it didn't take long before Leonidas's mind started questioning the loyalty of the people around him.

'Brother, if it wasn't you or me, then who the hell did this?'

'I don't know, it is likely we'll never find out.'

'Don't get me wrong, it saves us doing it but who would have the spine to assassinate a King outside of our plan?'

Leonidas knew this was something he wouldn't be able to assume, but it had questioned his trust. It is quite plausible

Cleombrotus, Gorgo, Isagoras, Cora, Cleisthenes, Leotychidas or the council could have reason for his killing.

Lycurgus stepped forward, 'Sorry to interrupt, we need to announce this to the rest of the council. I suggest we stick with death by self-mutilation.'

Leonidas gives a nod of approval and Lycurgus goes on his way.

'What is bothering you, brother, he's dead. This is what we wanted, remember? He never gave a shit about us.'

'Yes, this is true, but I know Cleomenes and he would have rather been murdered than take his own life. Now who can we trust?'

'I understand your concern, if someone can get this close to Cleomenes without us knowing, it could happen to us.'

Once the council had been informed of the suicide, Leonidas was officially made King of the Agiad dynasty. The path he believes the Gods had planned for him all along, has finally come to fruition.

Leotychidas confronted Leonidas, 'I'm sorry, Cleomenes brought shame to your dynasty but together we shall be a force to reckon with, he will soon be a distant memory.'

'Thank you. While you are here, I need you to make Gorgo my wife and Queen at the earliest opportunity.'

'Gorgo you say, as in Cleomenes's daughter?'

'Yes, after the disappointment of Cleomenes finding a suitable Queen and producing an heir. I do not wish to be compared to him.'

The Spartans considered their Kings to be priests of Zeus himself, therefore priests of the Spartan state were the Kings themselves, who were able to marry couples.

'Excellent,' says Leotychidas. 'The council will welcome such news.'

The following day, the council approves the marriage and no time is wasted. Gorgo is escorted to a room to perform the Spartan ritual of marriage.

Her hair is cut short and she is made to wear a Spartan cloak and sandals to resemble a man, a ritual intended to make the woman less intimidating.

Leonidas would spend the next few nights visiting Gorgo in the darkened room in secret and capture her in a ritual symbol of him abducting the woman he wishes to marry.

The purpose of this ritual is to make it tougher for new couples to consummate their marriage, this is to increase the desire between husband and wife, and encourage the creation of strong heirs.

Meeting in secret was nothing new to them and they are already aware, Eileithyia, the goddess of childbirth, has blessed them with an heir.

The ritual draws to a close and Leotychidas places a veil on Gorgo's newly cut hair. The veil is now an item she must wear daily as a married woman.

Leotychidas raises his hands in front of her, 'May the Gods bless you with fertility, health and beauty.'

The ceremony has now ended and they are officially married and the new King and Queen of Sparta.

Leonidas and Gorgo return to their favourite spot down by the Eurotus River. Leonidas uses this as his place to reflect and listen to the Gods; after all it, the river is a life line for Sparta providing water, food and defense.

'The Gods truly do favour us, Leonidas.'

'Yes, they do my Queen,' he says smiling, liking the sound of Gorgo as his Queen.

'I have something I want to share with you.'

'I'm listening.'

'My Father would have never let us been together, I believe he knew we were likely to have produced an heir before him, this would have posed a huge threat.'

'Yes, you are probably right. Ultimately, it would have placed him under more pressure from the elders.'

Gorgo embraces Leonidas tightly, mustering up the courage to get something off of her chest.

'That is why I did what I needed to, and you are now in your rightful position as King and I your Queen,' she whispers in his ear.to
 'Gorgo, what are you telling me?'
 'It was me, Leonidas; I killed my Father.'

17

Several years later, Leonidas has become a popular King; he has fulfilled his promise to Cleombrotus who is now his advisor and senior officer.

The Helot population has settled down and the threat of revolt is at a minimum.

Leonidas is bathing and making the most of his time to relax. Gorgo enters the room, 'My Queen, care to join me?' – she has a look of concern on her face – 'Something wrong?'

A messenger has arrived; he is being escorted here by Cleombrotus as we speak.

'Where is this messenger from?'

'Eryx, Sicily, Dorieus's colony.'

Leonidas immediately exits the water and get himself dressed. 'I'm surprised we have not heard from Dorieus sooner, no doubt he needs more resources,' he says, rolling his eyes.

When the messenger is escorted to the house Cleombrotus gives Leonidas a nod of approval to confirm he is safe and has no weapons. The messenger is filthy and has a deep wound on his leg, attracting the flies with its mild infection. It is quickly apparent something is wrong and that he isn't here to deliver good news.

'King Leonidas, it's a privilege' – the messenger respectfully bows – 'I am Deacon of Eryx, Sicily.'

'Did Dorieus send you?'

'No, I came on my own accord to deliver a message to you personally.'

'Please, speak freely as my guest.'

'It's Dorieus, he is dead. The colony was attacked by the Egestaeans who had support from the Carthaginians. Dorieus had a strong army but they were outnumbered and overwhelmed.'

Upon hearing the news, Leonidas didn't really know how to react, his relationship with either of his elder siblings was a complicated one. However, Dorieus was a brother by blood and that always carried a level of respect.

'Where is Dorieus now?'

'He was tortured then taken away to be murdered. He was later returned cut up in to dozens of pieces. They then held us as hostages and tortured us, as if it was a game.'

'Get Deacon cleaned up,' Leonidas instructed to Cleombrotus. 'You can stay here in Sparta and I will send a message to Sicily asking all the survivors to come to Sparta, it will be much safer for them here.'

'My King, that will not be possible, I was the only survivor as I managed to escape.'

'Everyone is dead?

'Yes, they butchered the entire army and slaughtered the women and children like livestock, all dead.' Cleombrotus escorts Deacon away.

'What are you going to do now? Gorgo asks.

Leonidas rubs his forehead as if trying to relieve a headache. 'I am not going to do anything. Retaliation from Sparta will not benefit us. We will only risk the lives of our men, unnecessarily.'

Leonidas turns to walk away but bumps in to a boy he didn't realise was standing so close behind him. Leonidas places his hand on the boy's head and ruffled his hair.

'I heard the messenger say someone called Dorieus is dead, who's that?' the boy asks.

Leonidas picks up the boy, 'Pleistarchus, my son, Dorieus was your uncle, my brother.'

Pleistarchus is a strong, energetic boy who is very intuitive. Leonidas believes he will make a good King one day with his adventurous streak and his desire to learn and copy his Father.

'Go play, boy, Cleombrotus will be back soon to show you how to fight,' says Leonidas, putting the boy down.

A short while later Cleombrotus returns.

'Great timing,' – Leonidas points to the courtyard – 'Pleistarchus is waiting to fight.'

'It will need to wait, the council require your presence at the Gerousia, Leotychidas is already on his way.'

Leonidas sighs, 'What is it now?'

'I am unsure, but everyone is in attendance.'

Upon their arrival at the Gerousia, there is a lot of commotion and heated conversations taking place. Lycurgus enters the Gerousia, his presence demands attention and the majority go silent.

'Silence while I speak please, we have plenty to address here today,' – he waits for silence throughout the Gerousia – 'some of you may or may not be aware that former King, Demaratus, has settled with the Persians.'

'Is that why we are here?' one of the elders asks.

'According to reports, Demaratus is now the advisor for King Xerxes.'

Leonidas turns to Cleombrotus, 'Well there's a shock,' he says, sarcastically.

Xerxes is the fourth King of the Achaemenid Empire; he is the son and successor of Darius the Great. His mother was daughter of Cyrus the Great, the first Achaemenid King. Since Demaratus was abdicated, Xerxes has amassed a massive army and navy as a delayed response to the defeat of the first Persian Invasion of Greece. This ended in an Athenian victory at the battle of Marathon, ten years earlier.

'Xerxes is starting a war based on his Father's defeat ten years ago and Demaratus is advising him?' Leotychidas wishes to confirm.

'They both clearly hold grudges,' says Leonidas, as the elders laugh in response to his sarcasm.

The threat is currently minimal, Xerxes army is reported to be in Hellespont, Turkey. It's believed the Persians will eventually cross Mount Olympus that borders between Thessaly and Macedonia, approximately two hundred and sixty miles North of Athens. It is a matter of time before they reach their destination.

Xerxes would be making a statement by crossing Mount Olympus, as all twelve Olympian Gods reside there. No mortals were allowed on the mountain, but Xerxes boasts he is the most powerful God of all and will prove this to his people when Zeus, the most powerful God of all, fails to strike him off of the mountain.

'How large is his army?' asks Leonidas.

'It is approximately two hundred and fifty thousand,' – he nervously gulps – 'and growing.'

An army of this size has never been heard of before; anyone who amasses a body of men that large wants complete domination.

Leotychidas appears agitated, 'We must strike now' – he clenches his fists – 'and hit them where it hurts when they least expect it. We have the resources and the men.'

The Ephors disagreed, by the time the Persians become close enough to be a real threat it will be August, time of the Carneia.

The Carneia is the great national traditional festival of Sparta, celebrating the God of flocks and herds, a festival of harvest. The festival is celebrated by Sparta every year between the seventh and fifteenth of August. All military operations are suspended during this time.

'We can manipulate the calendar,' suggested Leotychidas, desperate to attack sooner rather than later. 'Xerxes will storm through Mount Olympus, what makes you think he'll care about our festival?'

'The Gods will strike him down before he reaches this far,' replies Lycurgus.

'Then I hope you are right and the Gods favour us. Otherwise, Xerxes and by then, his half a million strong army, will trample straight through us.'

'One of Ephors stands to address the council, 'We will also be in an Olympic truce during this time.'

Leotychidas shakes his head in disagreement, 'Again' – sounding frustrated and banging his fist – 'this will not make the slightest bit of difference to someone like Xerxes. The size of his army reflects this.'

The Olympic truce is enacted to allow athletes and spectators to travel safely between cities and nations to participate in a series of athletic competitions held in honour of Zeus.

It is common for city states to use the competition as a political tool to assert dominance over their rivals and politicians to announce political alliances at the games.

'I must agree with Leotychidas, it is more than likely Xerxes will use this time to his advantage. We must delay him,' says Leonidas.

Leonidas was very aware of current political issues and what was being agreed between each city state. This would often leave the Ephors surprised, a sign that his understanding of current affairs was greatly underestimated. Leonidas was patient in his learning and has vowed to himself to learn from the previous mistakes his brothers had made, that they have paid costly for.

'Lycurgus, didn't you attend the congress of Greek city states last year when it was rumoured the Persian army was growing?'

'Yes, this is true.'

'It is also my understanding that the city states agreed to partner themselves against any potential forthcoming invasion. Sparta and Athens were foremost in this alliance, being sworn enemies of the Persians and acting on the truce we have established with them.'

'This is true too.'

Murmurs started amongst the council, 'Well, what was agreed? Surely this is relevant now there is a threat?' Leonidas had made a great point and Leotychidas was nodding in agreement.

Lycurgus lets out a sigh of breath, 'It was suggested, Sparta would command the land forces and the Athenian fleets would be commanded by Themistocles.'

Themistocles is an Athenian general and a non-aristocratic politician who has risen in popularity, having the support of lower-class Athenians and generally being at odds with the Athenian nobility.

'I do not see what's changed,' replies Leonidas.

'Your knowledge in current affairs impresses us all Leonidas, it shows great leadership. However, what you are unaware of is Aegina and Corinth refused to give command to the Athenians.'

'And the answer is in front of you Lycurgus,' says Leonidas, with a smug smile on his face.

Lycurgus glances around the council, 'Please, enlighten us.'

'Sparta can command the naval forces.' The council erupts in laughter. Sparta had an insignificant naval power that didn't create a huge threat, let alone one that would threaten Xerxes.

Lycurgus composed himself from laughing, 'What could we possibly demonstrate to them and the Athenians about naval warfare?'

There is a moment of silence as Leonidas thinks, 'We shall tell Aegina and Corinth we will command the fleets, then instantly hand the fleets over to Themistocles. They'll be none the wiser.'

The council remains silent at the suggestion, and then progressively each Ephor begins to nod in agreement.

'Very well, the congress meets again in the spring. However, the council will not approve any support if it's required during the Carneia, understood?'

'I understand,' replies Leonidas.

18

The following spring, Leonidas and Lycurgus travel to the congress of Greek city states, accompanied by Cleombrotus and Tiro.

Tiro's loyalty had not gone unnoticed and he had quickly become Leonidas's newly appointed polemarch, a senior military leader. They had come a long way since Leonidas's first day at the Agoge and were lifelong companions. With Cleombrotus as his senior advisor, Tiro was the logical choice to lead his army.

Upon their arrival they are greeted by Themistocles who is encouraged to see the Spartans in attendance. Leonidas and Themistocles had never met but they knew much about each other. It wouldn't take long before both of them struck a unique relationship, one of mutual respect.

The Greek city states didn't waste any time in deliberating over the risk of Persian invasion. It was abundantly clear the risk was imminent. With Athens and Sparta being the more dominant of nations among the congress, it was ultimately left to them.

Themistocles steps forward, 'I have already gained approval from Athens, that upon my request they are to build one hundred ships to increase our already superior fleet. I asked for more but this was rejected.'

'Why was this rejected?' asked a representative from Aegina.

'If the Persian army continue to progress, they'll arrive around August. This limits our timeframe to produce any more ships.'

The production of one hundred Athenian ships was encouraging for the city states to hear, knowing the Athenians had one of the most feared naval fleets in the world, their reputation exceeded them.

'What about the narrow Vale of Tempe?' – A Thessalian delegation nervously suggests – 'We have reliable sources that suggest Xerxes is sending a large advance army through there.'

The Vale of Tempe is a gorge in the Tempi municipality of northern Thessaly, Greece. It is located between Olympus to the north and Ossa to the south, and between the regions of Thessaly and Macedonia. The valley is ten kilometers long and as narrow as twenty-five meters in places, with cliffs nearly five hundred meters high. The Pineios River flows through it, all the way to the Aegean Sea. On the right bank of the Pineios is a temple to Apollo, where the laurels used to crown the victorious in the Pythian Games are gathered. They were held in honour of Apollo at his Delphi sanctuary every four years, two years after the Olympic Games.

'Why do you think he'll send an army through there?' asks Themistocles.

'The Thessalian people have witnessed numerous battles there throughout our history. The Tempe Pass is a strategic pass in Greece. It is the main route from Larisa through the mountains to the coast.'

'Why do I sense you are unsure?' says Leonidas.

The Thessalian nervously swallows, slightly intimidated by Leonidas's presence.

'It can be bypassed via the Sarantaporo Pass, but the alternative route takes longer.'

'Surely this is worth acting on, it'll be ideal as they'll reach here before the Carneia,' suggested Lycurgus. 'Let's vote, raise your hands if in agreement.'

Every city state raised their hand, the decision was unanimous.

'Then it's agreed, we'll intercept Xerxes army at the Tempe Pass.'

It was hoped that by crushing Xerxes army it would be a deterrent for him invading any further. Themistocles and Leonidas agree to supply ten thousand men in a strategy to overwhelm the Persians and demonstrate they are a force to be reckoned with.

'Who will command the Athenian Hoplites and Spartan Warriors?' asks Lycurgus, raising his eyebrows at Leonidas.

'Tiro will lead the ten thousand; the Thessalian people can assist him with their local knowledge of the terrain.'

'Thank you, my King.' This would be Tiro's first mission as the new polemarch, he was thirsty for blood in battle and he could think of no better way to prove himself but against the Persians.

Themistocles embraces Leonidas's arm to enforce his agreement, 'That's settled; I suggest we start making plans.'

Several weeks later, Themistocles and the Athenian army have marched north-west of the Attic Peninsula, where they meet the Spartan army, led by Tiro. The plan is to march the ten thousand north, then along the eastern coastal path to the Vale of Temp.

The journey was tough, especially along the coastal paths where the terrain can be challenging. As the army approached Thessalia, Tiro orders the army to pass west of Mount Ossa, recommended by Themistocles in the original plan. The terrain remains difficult but still far easier than passing the eastern side of the mountain.

The distant sound of the Pineios River could be heard, a welcomed sign after a hard march. The river was lined with dense trees and towering cliffs. They stopped to rest before making their way up river to the gorge; they used this time to collect water from a nearby spring.

'How much further is there to go?' Tiro asks one of the Thessalian guides, wiping the sweat from his brow.

'I would say at least half a day's march considering how dense the tree growth is. Before we come to the gorge, there should be a vast clearing where we can set up camp.'

Tiro nods and gives the order to march on.

The army eventually comes to a large clearing, but they are not alone.

The Spartans instantly unite to form their phalanx on Tiro's command, 'Identify yourselves or you'll fall where you stand.'

'I am Alexander the first of Macedon and the royal Argead dynasty, these are my men.'

Macedonia was a kingdom outside of the area dominated by the great city states of Athens, Sparta and Thebes.

'Why are you here?'

'I heard news your army would be passing here, but I come with warning.'

'And what might that be, Alexander of Macedon?' asks Tiro, approaching with his sword in hand.

'I have received threats from King Xerxes himself, stating his army will swallow my kingdom and anyone else that gets in his way.'

'We have received the same threat, that's why we are here,' replies Tiro. 'You travelled all this way to warn me of this?'

'No, I am suggesting you retreat.'

'Retreat, you must be mad!'

'I have sent out several scouts, two of which came back in pieces. However, one returned with news that Xerxes has amassed a much bigger army than initially thought.'

For Tiro, this changed nothing. He was there on orders to command the army and smash Xerxes advance. To retreat would mean to let down Leonidas and Sparta.

'I know of his army and we can take advantage of this position through that gorge.'

Alexander stepped closer, 'His army has become too large, in excess of five hundred thousand. Xerxes will not pass an army of that size through this gorge; he will by-pass it.'

'Sarantaporo Pass,' Tiro muttered to himself.

'Yes, you already know of this?'

'The Thessalians warmed us of this route.'

'Now I warn you, commander. Retreat, and find elsewhere to intercept his army.'

Tiro became frustrated; he wanted this opportunity to prove himself in battle, there is no better death than in the name of Sparta or to return home victorious.

Tiro and Themistocles decide to camp for the night, their men were restless and Themistocles wanted to use his time to muster up a new strategy.

They both sit silently around an open fire. The therapeutic sound of the river can be heard and the moon is bright. The night sky displays billions of stars and despite a massive Persian invasion looming; a sense of tranquility is in the air.

'I've been thinking. Why don't we intercept Xerxes at Sarantaporo Pass?' Tiro says to Themistocles, who is deep in thought and takes a moment before responding.

'No, we will not hold any advantages there. An army of that size will walk straight through us.'

'Then what the fuck do you suggest, Themistocles?

'We retreat.'

'I will not retreat, nor can you force me to,' replies Tiro, angrily.

'No, but I can force your hand. Tomorrow morning, I will be returning to Athens with my men. To not follow me would be suicide.'

'What, you can't do that.'

'I can and when I return and hear news of you and your men being unnecessarily slaughtered, I will make it common knowledge that you ignored the advice of an experienced general.'

'You're a coward, bastard.' Tiro stands up in frustration kicking the dust from the ground in to the fire, causing the ambers to violently disperse.

'I promise you we'll come up with a new plan; you will spill the blood of Persians, that I can assure you.'

'That doesn't change the fact this has been a disaster and we have spent days marching ten thousand men for no fucking reason.' Tiro walked away to go get some sleep before sunrise. It took him some time before he was able to drift off to sleep, the day's events going around in his mind.

With the Persian army imminently approaching, the Greeks needed a new plan, and fast.

19

Back in Sparta, Tiro has returned home and is de-briefing Leonidas on the events.

'Tiro, I understand your frustration but I have to agree with Themistocles,' says Leonidas, reassuring Tiro made the right decision.

'The decision doesn't sit well with me, my King.'

'As a Spartan I understand what you mean, it just wasn't your time yet. It will come. You are a good friend who doesn't need to demonstrate his loyalty.'

Within days, Leonidas receives a message from Themistocles informing him Xerxes is now through the Hellespont and that he has a new plan.

Hellespont is a narrow, natural strait and significant waterway that forms part of the boundary between Greece and Asia. Hellespont also connects the Sea of Marmara with the Aegean and Mediterranean Seas.

Fortunately, for the Greeks, Xerxes has suffered delays at the Hellespont. It took Xerxes several attempts to cross due to the size of his army. His army was so massive he requested two bridges to be built at Abydos. However, both crossings could not withstand the storms or the strong tides and the bridges ended up being destroyed.

News travelled fast that Xerxes ordered the execution of the Egyptian and Phoenician engineers that designed the bridges and had their heads tossed in to the sea. To demonstrate his supposed authority over the Gods, Xerxes took it upon himself to punish the sea by throwing fetters into the strait; given it three hundred lashes and branded it with a red-hot iron while his soldiers shouted at the water. Xerxes kept one engineer alive who suggested he tied all his ships together from Abydos to Sestos, eventually allowing his army to successfully cross.

Themistocles's second strategy was protecting the route to southern Greece. Xerxes would require his army to travel through the very narrow pass.

'Where is this pass, he mentions?' requests Cleombrotus.

'Thermopylae,' answers Leonidas.

Themistocles claims this could easily be blocked by the Greeks, despite the overwhelming number of Persians; furthermore, Themistocles confirms to prevent the Persians bypassing Thermopylae by sea, the Athenian and allied navies will block the straits of Artemisium.

'I'm not sure about this strategy, are you sure you want to march our army out from the Peloponnesus, again?' asks a concerned Tiro.

'I must admit, I have my doubts after Themistocles was so keen to retreat before.'

To persuade the Spartans to defend Attica, Themistocles would need to show them that the Athenians were willing to do everything necessary for the success of the alliance. To be taken seriously, Themistocles must persuade the entire Athenian fleet to be dispatched to Artemisium.

Cleombrotus looks perplexed, 'Themistocles has a huge task ahead. What is the likelihood he persuades Athens to deploy their entire fleet?'

'He informs me he will confirm this as soon as he can at the forthcoming meeting with ally city states, so we have no choice but to wait.'

'Agreed, but we have our own problem. . . The Carneia must be honoured.'

That evening, Leonidas is thinking how he can persuade the council to delay the Carneia, already knowing Lycurgus will not approve of such a thing. For the first time, Leonidas feels torn and confused over his duty. He has sworn to protect Sparta at all costs, yet it is Sparta that is preventing him from doing so.

Gorgo can see something is weighing on the Kings mind; she approaches Leonidas and starts to massage his neck and shoulders. The King closes his eyes and relaxes his shoulders, instantly benefiting from the relief of Gorgo's hands.

'What is on your mind?' she asks.

'The Persians are advancing while we sit here and wait. They have an army bigger than anything this world has ever seen. Yet the Carneia must be honoured, potentially sacrificing not just all of Sparta, but all of Greece.'

'What does your gut tell you?'

'My gut tells me I must protect Sparta, at all costs.'

'Trust in the Gods, Leonidas. If you protect Sparta and die in its name, how could that possibly displease them?' Gorgo gives Leonidas a kiss and leaves to check on Pleistarchus.

Leonidas gazes in to the night from his balcony, muttering to the Gods for help.

A gentle thud is heard above Leonidas's head, as he notices a shadow cast on to the balcony floor. As he slowly turns, he notices a white owl on the rooftop, clenching a dead field mouse in its talons. He observes the owl using its hooked beak to tear in to its prey. He smiles as he reminisces on the first time, he paid attention to the white owl.

'Tuto, are you still watching over me?' he says out loud. Startled, the owl takes flight with a single swoop of its wings.

The first time Leonidas saw the owl during his time in the Agoge, he was fascinated by its reliance and poise. Thereafter, he always considered the owl as a sign from the Gods. *'This must have been a sign from the Gods, for the owl to show up tonight, of all nights,'* he thought.

Meanwhile, in Athens, discussions with the assembly are progressing late in to the night. Themistocles must convince all Athenian politicians, that in order to convince Sparta Athens needs to deploy their entire naval fleet. This means every able-bodied Athenian male would be required to man the ships. Themistocles has always had a way with words, his speech was vivifying and it gripped the assembly from the onset.

Themistocles began to close his speech. 'If there is a time to listen to me, listen to me now. The threat of Persian invasion is real, our entire nation will burn, your wives, your children will be tortured and raped then thrown in to the burnt ruins of our beloved city,' – he pauses momentarily to observe their body language – 'we must prepare to abandon Athens. Women and children will be sent to the city of Troezen, the Argolid Peninsula, safely inside the Peloponnesus. By all means prove me wrong. If not, you must approve of my proposal if this state is to survive.'

There was nothing more Themistocles could say, he had given it his all and it was now left to the vote.

It was unlikely such an audacious proposal would be accepted. A proposal of this magnitude had never been pulled off before, but then the threat of an army of this scale was also a first. Themistocles was an ambitious individual; it was this ambition that many feared, but it was also this ambition that many followed.

After a short wait the vote was announced. A unanimous decision was made to approve the proposal. Themistocles could not believe he has pulled it off; it was a momentous occasion for him and Athens. During a time where the Athenian people were facing their biggest threat to date, committed themselves to the words of Themistocles to save them.

With his proposals accepted, Themistocles wasted no time in issuing the orders for the women and children of Athens to be sent to the city of Troezen. Some citizens refused to leave the city so their fate will now be left to the Gods. Themistocles then travels to the meeting with the ally city states, where he will propose his strategy; with the Athenian fleet fully committed to the defense of Greece, he now needed the ally states to accept his proposal.

It did not take much for any of the ally city states to agree with Themistocles. The majority knew without Athens naval fleet none of them would stand a chance, and they were willing to fight for their land. They waited in anticipation to hear his plan on the strategy the armies will need to adopt.

'You know I am with you on this, Themistocles, but we have a very big problem,' Leonidas says, with a slight tone of distress in his voice.

'Ah yes, the Carneia.' Themistocles rolls his eyes in frustration.

'We have spoken briefly on Thermopylae, it's a good plan but it is not me you need to convince. I suggest you travel back to Sparta with me and propose this plan to the council.'

'I will gladly address your council; we must do so as soon as possible; time is of the essence.'

They wasted no time and with haste, the Spartans made their way back to Sparta with Themistocles by their side.

Upon their return to Sparta, Leonidas and his peers addressed the council with Themistocles.

'Themistocles, what do we owe the pleasure?' asks Lycurgus.

Leonidas attempts to answer on his behalf but is instantly stopped by Lycurgus.

Themistocles knew his proposal would take some convincing.

'As you are aware council, Xerxes and his huge army are moving fast and before long we will all be under Persian command, or dead, with any luck.'

Lycurgus smirks at Themistocles. 'You've travelled a long way to tell me something we already know; I believe you have a proposal?'

'Yes, in order for my navy to be successful and for our land to be safe, we need Spartan strength and numbers in the phalanx' – Themistocles pauses for a moment, he checks he still has their attention – 'we need Sparta to lead the way on land and block the pass at Thermopylae.'

There was some commotion within the council; Themistocles could hear the words Carneia and Olympics muttered amongst the conversations.

'No, Athenian, by the time Xerxes and his army arrives the Carneia will be in full swing. This request is simply out of the question.'

'Please, consider your actions here today could be responsible for the downfall of Greece. If the Spartans do no hold Thermopylae, my navy cannot succeed at Artemisium,' he said with frustration.

Lycurgus can see Themistocles is angry and frustrated at their stubbornness to fight during the Carneia.

'I will consult the Oracle, Themistocles, but do not expect a different answer. Until then, no longer speak of such a plan.'

The council disperse and Leonidas approaches Themistocles, 'Please stay as my guest, feast with us tonight and tomorrow the council can disclose what the Oracle has said.'

Themistocles accepts and awaits the council's response, but he does not hold his breath for the response he is hoping for.

A short time later, the words of the Oracle are being reverberated around the Gerousia.

'For you, inhabitants of Sparta, either your city gets destroyed and wasted by Persian men, or Lacedaemon must mourn a dead King. The might and strength of a Lion will not restrain him as he has the might of Zeus.'

'That settles it,' confirmed Lycurgus. 'Sparta will not join you in this fight. We will protect our city should we need to and if the Persians make it this far, so be it.'

The council was adjourned; Themistocles was outraged by the decision and degree of stubbornness displayed. He stormed out of the Gerousia, making arrangements to immediately return to Athens.

Leotychidas looks over to Leonidas, 'What can we do?' he says, shrugging his shoulders.

Suddenly, Leonidas had a thought. A decision he believes will leave a legacy for generations. He indicates for Cleombrotus and Tiro to follow him, soon catching up with Themistocles.

'Themistocles,' shouts Leonidas, grabbing his attention.

Themistocles stops and waits for them to catch up, 'I must say Leonidas, I thought more highly of Sparta.'

'Forget that nonsense my Athenian friend, I don't always listen to them. Promise me one thing?' he asks with a devilish smile.

'Go on.'

'Make sure you have your navy ready, Athenian.' They shake hands enthusiastically before seeing Themistocles off.

'Leonidas,' calls Themistocles, nearly disappearing out of sight; 'don't be late.'

Leonidas responds with a single nod of his head then walks back in to the city, instructing Cleombrotus and Tiro of their responsibilities. Tiro would be responsible for selecting three hundred of their best Spartan warriors; due to the Carneia, resources would be tight.

'If possible, only select those of the royal guard who have at least one son, the preservation of Sparta is reliant on its warriors, this is crucial,' instructs Leonidas.

Leonidas instructs Cleombrotus to remain in Sparta to raise and mentor his son, Pleistarchus.

'I would love nothing more than to fight alongside you, brother. I would be lying if I said it doesn't disappoint me. However, I understand the importance of mentoring Pleistarchus. I assure you; he is in the best of hands.'

Leonidas places his hand on Cleombrotus's shoulder, 'I don't doubt it for a second, brother. With your guidance he will one day make a fine leader, this is why I chose you.'

They were now on a tight deadline to get their affairs in order, Xerxes was making relatively good progress but wasn't without his own challenges and delays.

News was travelling fast that Xerxes and his imperial army were picking up the pace, setting ablaze every dwelling and town along the way. Scorching his mark through Greece there were few states willing to get in his way. The ones that tried were wiped clean from the face of the Earth.

Leonidas was unaware of the progress Xerxes was making. He was at home spending time with his family, telling Pleistarchus the legendary Spartan story of the Battle of Champions.

No sooner than he finished telling the story, Tiro approached. The time has come for Leonidas to leave, it was earlier than expected but he didn't question it. Tiro has assembled the men on the outskirts of the city where they await their orders.

Tiro waited outside so Leonidas could say his farewell. He went to speak but was stopped from doing so by Gorgo. She felt torn between her love for Leonidas and their duty to Sparta. She kissed the King gently on his lips and embraced him, turning towards his ear she whispers, 'Come back with your shield, or on it.'

'My lady,' he acknowledged, tightening their embrace.

'What should I do if you do not return?'

'You marry a good man and have good children.'

Pleistarchus brought over his shield; it was nearly as big as him.

'Thank you, my son,' – Leonidas affectionately squeezes his shoulder and pats the palm of his hand on his cheek – 'take care of your mother and serve Sparta well.'

Pleistarchus remained silent; he was too young to understand the magnitude of the forthcoming events.

Gorgo was momentarily day dreaming as she contemplated the potential outcome of Leonidas going to war, and then he was gone. Gorgo and Pleistarchus rushed to the door to get a final glimpse of him leave with Tiro.

'With your shield or on it,' Gorgo muttered to herself.

Leonidas and Tiro had reached the outskirts of the city where the Spartan royal guard was waiting. Cleombrotus has met them there to see them off.

'These are fine looking soldier's, Tiro,' Leonidas says with an impressed look on his face.

'Three hundred of the best my King, as requested, all with at least one son left behind to continue their name and Sparta's legacy.'

'Thank you, Tiro.'

Leonidas walked down the line of men looking in to their eyes, he could see the fire in their souls and their burning desire to fight and if required, die an honourable death.

The King approaches Alec, who has a very serious facial expression, a look of determination and loyalty. Leonidas returns the same look, both cracking a smile.

'It's good to have you here, Alec. I feel sorry for the Persians.'

Leonidas turns to face Cleombrotus; they embrace and put their heads together.

'Your years of loyalty have exceeded you, brother. Thank you for standing by my side.'

Cleombrotus gives Leonidas a firm pat on both shoulders, 'Pleistarchus is in good hands until your return.'

Leonidas smiles, 'I appreciate the optimism, brother.'

A familiar voice speaks out; it's Lycurgus and his noblemen. 'At first I doubted the rumours; Leonidas would not disobey the council and Oracle. Tell me you are not planning to face Xerxes with these men.'

Leonidas laughs out loud, 'Sure, I am not planning to face Xerxes with these men,' he sarcastically replies.

'Then what is this?'

'I am planning to face Xerxes with these soldiers!' he shouts with emphasis, followed by the battle chant of three hundred Spartans.

'The Gods will curse you for this blasphemy; the Carneia is in full swing.'

'Curse me for protecting Sparta? Unlikely' – Leonidas looks up to the sky as if addressing the Gods – 'it appears they do not have anything to say.'

Leonidas nods at Tiro who immediately orders the command to leave, the Spartans simultaneously about-turn and start to march. Leonidas pays one last tribute to Cleombrotus with a bow of his head, then follows on with his men.

Lycurgus looks at Cleombrotus for some kind of explanation, shaking his head in disbelief.

Cleombrotus returns the look with a smug grin and a shrug of his shoulders.

'Fuck,' says Lycurgus, kicking the ground in anger.

20

The Spartans begin their march, estimated to take approximately three days. This should put them just ahead of Xerxes and give them the opportunity to prepare for battle.

The weather was fair and the terrain was kind, this allowed Leonidas and his men to progress, further making good time.

After a solid day of marching, the Spartans set up camp for the night. The mood was relaxed, conversations continued in to the night with occasional laughter being heard. Eventually, the majority got their heads down for some sleep and it wasn't long before the camp fell silent.

Leonidas lay looking up to the stars thinking of Gorgo and Pleistarchus, he knew deep down he would not see them again.

A loud popping noise from the nearby camp fire interrupted his thoughts, the orange glow from the flames gently highlighting the surrounding trees, casting large shadows across the clearing, where they lay.

Leonidas was drawn in by the flames, their appearance hypnotic and somewhat soothing to observe. Something then caught Leonidas's attention as he starred through the flames and in to the tree line ahead. Perched on a branch under a small canopy of leaves was the image of an owl. Leonidas strongly believes this to be the same owl that has become symbolic throughout his life. He doesn't believe in coincidence; this was another sign from the Gods.

Leonidas peered through the flames looking in to its eyes that appeared a deep orange, reflecting the flames from the fire, creating the illusion its eyes were ablaze.

The owl swooped off, silhouetting itself against the backdrop of a clear full moon. Leonidas always saw the owl as a good sign and it gave him a sense of reassurance that he is doing the right thing, even if he was to die.

The following morning moments before sunrise, Tiro and Leonidas are the first up as they observe the sun just starting to rise over the horizon. An intense ray of light beams across the land, highlighting the true beauty of Greece and emphasising exactly what it is they are willing to defend and die for.

'We have a long day ahead of us, Tiro. We need to keep moving,' Leonidas orders.

'Yes, my King.' He steps over the men, giving them a kick as he passes.

The weather remains warm and the terrain is becoming increasingly challenging to navigate as they pass through some deep valleys, where they expect to be joined by further support towards the end of the day.

The days marching was going to plan, the landscape has become more exposed and easier to travel along. Leonidas has guided his men in good time and they are on track to enter Thermopylae the following day.

'My King, look over there,' Alec cries out, pointing to the horizon on the west.

Leonidas raised his arm to indicate the Spartans to halt.

'Spartans, halt,' ordered Tiro.

The Spartans come to an abrupt halt and wait further command while Leonidas observes a body of men in the clearings ahead.

'Who is it, my King?' Tiro asks.

'That my friend, is the Phocians and Locrians; I anticipated we would meet them in these regions.'

The Phocians were tribes from Phocis, a region of central Greece, north of the Gulf of Corinth. The Locrians are from Locris, also a tribe from central Greece and are closely related to the Phocians and Dorians.

The Phocians had good knowledge of Thermopylae; they had fought there before and had built a defensive wall that partly remained intact.

'Their numbers look strong, my King,' Tiro says, with a sense of relief.

'Yes, up to two thousand I believe, they will be vital in our defense and we will use the Phocians to prevent our enemy outflanking us.'

The tribes eventually joined Leonidas and the three hundred Spartans. It was reassuring to see their numbers increase in support for their cause but Leonidas knew in his gut it wouldn't be enough. This was going to be a mission to delay the Persians, rather than defeat them.

They settle down for their final night before arriving at Thermopylae, the following day. Leonidas discusses tactics with the Phocian leader who explains about the Phocian wall and its advantages.

'Please, tell me more,' Leonidas requests, wanting to be fully prepared upon arrival, not knowing the progress Xerxes is making.

'The best advantage is for us to make a stand at the middle gate,' the Phocian suggests.

'The middle gate, ok.'

'Yes, this is the narrowest part of the pass and the Persians will have no choice but to approach us with limited numbers.'

'And how do you recommend we use the wall?'

'Upon our arrival we must stack the wall higher. The wall is just in front of the middle gate.'

Leonidas confidently nods at the Phocians suggestions. 'So, we can use the wall for defense but it will also force the Persians towards our phalanx.'

'Exactly, then we'll stack the wall higher using the Persian corpses.'

'Excellent, my friend. Let's get some rest now. Tomorrow is going to be another long day.'

Leonidas is restless, going over as many scenarios as he could in his mind. He would have an advantage in the narrow pass of the hot gates but he questioned himself for how long. It would be a matter of time before they are overwhelmed with Xerxes numbers.

'We must hold that pass for as long as we can, at least so the remaining Greeks can assemble their armies,' he thought to himself.

The following morning felt like it came quicker than normal. The Spartans and their allies were stretching off their tight leg muscles, due to the distances they have marched in the last few days. Fortunately, they were all still in exceptional condition and eager to get in to battle.

There was no tension in the air, just excitement at the opportunity to be able to defend Greece and slay the Persians. Alec and some of the other Spartans were already making bets on who would have the biggest body count.

'I think we know who that'll be,' Alec said, with a confident smirk, tapping his finger on the point of his dagger.

'Ok, if you think so,' replies a fellow Spartan.

'I do actually, I'll get more than you. I can assure you of that, Aristodemus.'

Aristodemus was a trusted Spartan amongst the ranks; he was highly respected as a senior soldier who had been through his fair share of battles. If anyone wanted a Spartan by their side, it was Aristodemus.

The Spartans and allies covered good ground in the morning, making their way north east towards the coastal path. The march was becoming increasingly challenging with various levels of terrain and small valleys to pass through before the opening stretch to the pass.

The sound of the sea could be heard at the final elevation, the distant sound of the waves crashing against the coastline was a welcome sound.

Leonidas halted the armies before descending down the final hillside. He embraced the sun and the ocean breeze on his face, cooling the sweat on his brow.

From the top of the hill Leonidas could just make out the Greek navy, left in the trusted hands of Themistocles to block the straits of Artemisium, preventing Xerxes using his navy to by-pass the Spartans at Thermopylae.

Tiro joined Leonidas at the top to take in the view. 'Well, my King, looks like we are here, at last' – Tiro was curious as to what Leonidas was observing, so he follows his line of sight – 'Shit! Is that what I think it is?'

Leonidas nods, 'That is Xerxes army.'

They could see an army so vast that from a distance it took the appearance of a huge swarm of insects completely engulfing the coastline.

'The rumours were true, my King. The biggest army ever assembled,' Tiro states.

Leonidas smiles and turns Tiro around. On the lower coastal path there were large numbers of ally Greek forces waiting for Leonidas's arrival. They included, Demophilus, Commander of at least seven hundred Thespians. The Thebans had also arrived for battle; despite their numbers being small, Leonidas was grateful for their presence.

He now had the support of approximately seven thousand men from surrounding ally states.

'Tiro, ready the men.'

'Yes, my King, what are your orders?'

'March in to the hot gates.'

21

Leonidas wastes no time in strategically setting up their defenses, remembering all the advice and guidance Themistocles and the Phocian Commander recommended.

The Thespians had already started to hastily rebuild the Phocian wall, the plan is to make it at least six feet high but time was not on their side.

One thousand allied Greeks have been sent to the hilltop to block a path that could potentially be used to outflank their position. The Phocians along with the Thespians are to guard the wall and prevent a breach.

Tiro had briefed the Spartans on Leonidas's orders; they are to defend the narrowest part of the pass between the wall and the coastline, occasionally rotating to prevent fatigue.

The remaining Greeks were split to defend the rear, in case they are outflanked and the rest to contribute at the front line. This includes fighting, clearing the dead, treating the wounded and logistical tasks such as food and water replenishment.

The stage was set and it was now a waiting game for Xerxes forces to attack, while they wait the Spartans prepared themselves for battle.

The Spartans stripped down from their armour and prepared their bodies with oils, combed their hair and fixed it in position for battle. This was all in preparation not just for battle but for their deaths.

'I suggest you start exercising, get your bodies prepared for combat,' Tiro commands, jumping and bringing his knees up to his chest.

Unbeknown to Leonidas, Xerxes and his imperial army had arrived at Anthela, west of the pass where they camped, five days ago.

Xerxes had no choice but to wait, a third of his navy had been destroyed in a vicious storm off the coast of Magnesia and they needed time to regroup and catch up. Xerxes was confident once his navy arrived, they would obliterate Themistocles's ships, taking away the Greeks advantage of holding the pass at Thermopylae. Despite Xerxes losing a third of his ships, he still had a force of twelve hundred ships remaining.

At camp, Xerxes has had an enormous throne built draped in lace and gold in order for him to observe his army defeat the Greeks.

'Bring me a horseman to spy on the Greeks,' Xerxes demands, clapping his hands in haste.

'Yes, King of Kings.'

The spy arrives promptly.

'I am confident my army outnumbers the enemy; however, I need to know how many hoplites are waiting on the other side of that pass, behind that wall.'

'As you wish my King,' says the spy.

'Bring me any other findings you believe of benefit.'

The spy bows and gracefully turns to leave.

A while later, the horseman returns with a perplexed look on his face. 'Well, what did you see?' asks Xerxes, sitting forward on his throne in anticipation.

'I've never seen anything like it, my King. They are playing with each other's hair, stripping to exercise and laughing, like they are enjoying themselves.'

'What about their numbers?'

'Hard to say for sure, a few thousand; small in comparison to your forces, my King.'

Xerxes took reassurance in knowing this. 'Find me a messenger to deliver this message to Leonidas.'

'Yes, my King,' replies one of his servants.

'Tell Leonidas, if they surrender to me, their God King, I will spare their lives and they will remain free men under my reign. I will also donate them land that belonged to those who refused to surrender.'

'Yes, my King,' the servant confirms, gulping nervously at the thought of Leonidas's response.

Xerxes was apprehensive and wasn't expecting the Spartans to agree, particularly after the events of his Father, Darius.

A short while later, the messenger approaches the wall requesting to speak with their leader, King Leonidas.

Leonidas was intrigued and agreed to hear the messenger out, warning him that he is responsible for what he is about to say.

The messenger relayed the information to Leonidas who couldn't help but laugh. 'The God King?' he's confident, I'll give him that.'

Leonidas pulled out his sword and held it to the messenger's neck.

'Please, I am just the messenger, if you kill me who will you send back to return your message?' the messenger nervously pleads for his life.

'Who said anything about returning a message?' ask Leonidas.

With a single swipe of his sword, he took off his head, the body instantly becoming limp and collapsing to the floor, blood squirting over Leonidas's feet and soaking in to the sand.

The remaining men that accompanied the messenger all stepped back, as they became outnumbered by approaching Spartans.

Xerxes is outraged by the news, spitting with rage as he shouts and curses Leonidas and his men. He orders the surviving men who returned to be executed immediately.

'Cowards, may this be a lesson to you and anyone else who cowers away from our enemy.'

Several contingents of the Peloponnesians, including the Corinthians and Phlians, question Leonidas's reaction. Afraid of the number of Persians they face, they suggest abandoning Northern Greece and fall back to the Isthmus.

Leonidas did not take kindly to their suggestion. 'What good will that do?' – They look around at one another, but nobody was bold enough to respond – 'Either you die here making a stand and a difference, or run back to your homes and explain to your children and your wives you abandoned your duty. Only to have Xerxes men invade your state much sooner, raping and murdering your loved ones because they didn't have enough time to evacuate, thanks to you.'

The Phocians confidently re-confirm their allegiance to Leonidas. 'We stand by your side, Leonidas, 'til the end!' one of them shouts.

The Locrians step forward, acknowledging their support. Both the Locrians and the Phocians are aware of the importance of their presence, as their states are still evacuating.

The Corinthians and Phlians reluctantly decide to remain at Thermopylae.

Aristodemus snarls at their commanders, 'Cowards, the lot of you. Only ever interested in cooperating if it suits your region.'

Leonidas pats Aristodemus on the back. 'It's fine, brother. Go help Tiro finish preparing our men. I am expecting a reaction from Xerxes soon, we need to be ready.'

'Yes, my King.'

A short while later, Leonidas and his men were ready for battle and in position. The Phocians and Thespians situated in front of the hastily reconstructed wall.

'My King, it appears the Persians are advancing towards us,' states Tiro, from an observation point.

Not all of Xerxes troops had arrived in Thermopylae, Xerxes decided he had been waiting long enough and orders five thousand of his archers to rain a colossal barrage of arrows on to the Greeks. This was Xerxes way of providing them with a taste of his power.

Their numbers were so large the archers could be clearly heard placing their arrows simultaneously on to their bows and the sound of five thousand bowstrings being pulled back to full stretch.

'Shields!' commands Tiro.

The allied Greeks reiterate the same command passing it along the pass.

The Spartans gather tightly together in their phalanx, all their shields interlocking together to avoid any chance of penetration.

The archers release their bowstrings, creating a high pitch whistle as thousands of arrows fill the sky creating a huge arch of darkness. As the arrows close in on their targets, the air temperature momentarily cools as the arrows block the sun from shining through.

Many of the arrows land short creating a thudding noise that quickly becomes louder as they approach the Spartans, slamming against their shields. Leonidas orders the Spartans to maintain their composure and hold their position. The order is barely heard with the constant noise of the arrows smashing in to their shields and piercing through the bronze outer layer.

Distant screams of Greeks from allied states could be heard. The defence of some of the allied Greeks was not as strong as the Spartans. Several hoplites receive arrows through the neck and head, the force of the arrow knocking them to their backs.

Suddenly, after what seems like an attack that will never end, there is silence; apart from the odd whistle of an arrow delayed on its release.

Tiro orders them to stand and evaluate any damage or deaths.

The Spartans stand, they have sustained zero injuries. The bombardment of arrows proved to be relatively ineffective.

'Persian Cowards,' says Leonidas, as he pulls the arrows out that pin his cloak to the ground.

Their shields and the ground around them are littered with arrows. Some of the Greeks that possess bows start collecting the arrows to use as their own.

Once clearing their shields, they prepare themselves for another imminent attack.

Xerxes was far from finished, his next move was to send a force of ten thousand Medes, a population that inhabited an area called Media, between Western and Northern Iran. The ten thousand included support from the Cissians. Xerxes tasks them to take the Greeks prisoner and bring them before him.

'By nightfall I want Leonidas's head by my feet,' the King demands.

The Persians waste no time launching a frontal assault, a wave of ten thousand men make haste towards the Greek position.

The Greeks organised themselves in front of the Phocian wall, fewer soldiers are required as they are at the narrowest part of the pass.

The Spartans waited in their phalanx, their shields interlocked together, heads low and spears ready.

'Protect your neighbour, fight for Sparta and your honour,' Leonidas demands.

'Hold firm!' orders Tiro, as Xerxes troops close in.

Xerxes men pause within one hundred yards of the Spartans. Their numbers now seeming irrelevant, they only have as many men as they can fit across the pass, each one of them facing a Spartan thirsty for blood.

'Drop your weapons!' orders a Persian.

'Come and get them, Persians!' replies Leonidas, defiantly.

Xerxes troops advance, sprinting towards the Spartans in a free for all charge.

Tiro can hear his breathings increase within his helmet, his heart beat increasing immensely, practically beating against the inside of his breastplate as his body fills with adrenaline.

'Slice them to pieces, Spartans. No Mercy,' Leonidas says, motivating his men, itching to make contact with the enemy.

Xerxes troops smash in to the Spartan phalanx, the first row of men bouncing off of the shields as if running in to a fortress wall. The Spartans barely move, only slightly adjusting their footing to maintain the phalanx.

The next wave of troops fails to make any significant impact as they crash to the floor, allowing the Spartans to finish them quickly, plunging their spears in to their chests or through their heads, making certain no man is left alive.

Xerxes observes the battle from a distance sat in his throne, standing up in frustration as he watches the Spartans slice down his men with ease.

Xerxes troops are poorly equipped, their spears are shorter and their shields are made from wicker.

The Spartans make easy work of their enemy, slicing straight through their shields and in to their chest cavities. Their armour was no defense against a spear with the force of a Spartan behind it.

Xerxes men could see no way through the Spartan phalanx, they start to panic as they are forced in to the pass. In an act of desperation, some of them decide to jump over the first row of Spartans, only to land on the end of the next spear.

'Forward!' Leonidas orders.

The Spartans trample over the heaps of dead bodies, finishing off the few that are still alive.

Vast numbers of Xerxes men begin to retreat, the Spartans break the phalanx to pursue the enemy along with the Thespians and Phocians.

They move swiftly through Xerxes men, striking them down in waves. The floor area is covered with maimed corpses, severed arms, legs and heads. Any remaining ground space is soaked in blood.

Xerxes jumps off of his throne in anger, cursing his soldiers for their incompetence, it was a blood bath.

The first major battle draws to a close. 'Aristodemus, count the dead and treat the wounded,' requests Leonidas.

'I'll get food and water distributed, my King,' says Alec.

The Thespians approach Leonidas, 'What about their dead, should we clear the ground?'

Leonidas ponders for a moment and smiles, 'Yes, clear the dead and stack them along the wall. That should improve our defenses.'

Aristodemus returns a short time later, 'We have lost five Spartan men, my King. Some minor injuries sustained too, but nothing serious.'

'They died a perfect death,' replies Leonidas, nodding his head with satisfaction.

'The kind of death we can only dream of, for now,' says Aristodemus.

'As for minor injuries, how is your eye?' asks Leonidas, pointing to the severe cut he notices across the eyelid.

'Nothing but a lucky thrust of a spear, my King. The culprit is around here, somewhere,' acknowledging the vast number of dead.

'Get it treated, I need you fit and well.'

Aristodemus nods in agreement then seeks medical attention.

'Tiro, order the rotation of the Greek allies to prevent fatigue. Make it quick,' observing the activity of Xerxes army.

'Looks like we are in for a long day,' says one of the Phocians, taking a moment to rest.

To Leonidas's surprise, Xerxes has sent another messenger who approaches on horseback.

The messenger is respectful and bows to Leonidas.

'I have an offering from the King of Kings, the great Xerxes.'

Leonidas smiles, folding his arms with an intrigued look upon his face.

'You do know what happened to your last messenger, don't you? he's somewhere in that wall.'

The messenger looks over to the wall and vomits down the side of his horse.

The Spartans laugh hysterically before Leonidas silences them, raising his hand, 'Go on with your message, Persian.'

'Surrender now and your homes will not be torched to the ground and your women and children will live another day. If you answer no, then you will face the wrath of the Immortals in all their glory.'

'Well, it looks like we have done alright so far, Persian. Perhaps you should be the ones to surrender. By all means, send these Immortals, I was thinking of building another wall on that side of the pass.'

'Do not be foolish, Spartan.'

Suddenly, a Spartan spear glides through the air slamming in to the messenger's eye, exiting out of the back of his head. His body slides off the horse, landing in an awkward heap on the ground, twitching. The horse startles and gallops off, stomping over the messenger as he tumbles beneath its hooves and becomes entangled in its legs. The horse kicks out its back legs, kicking the messenger and spear clear. The horse pauses for a moment and then blows through its lips before galloping off.

Tiro dusts off his hands after throwing the spear, 'That's one less Persian.'

'Well, that ended that conversation,' says Leonidas.

Back at the Persian camp, Xerxes notices the horse return covered in blood, with no messenger.

Xerxes reflects on the advice given to him from the former King of Sparta, Demaratus, now siding with the Persians.

'Before you leave for Thermopylae my King, a word of advice. Do not underestimate the Spartans, they have lived and trained their entire lives, for this very moment. They will never surrender.'

Furious, he commands the Immortals to immediately attack, confident they will not survive the wave of Immortals.

The Spartans observe the Immortals approach, the thundering noise of ten thousand men marching in step with one another was an intimidating site to behold.

The Spartans remain composed.

The Immortals already have a formidable reputation, that gave them a psychological edge over most of their enemies. If one was to die in battle, they were instantly replaced, the dead are cleared as quickly as possible giving the impression they are immortal.

Heavily armoured, all ten thousand are in possession of bow and arrows, a long-curved dagger, a short spear six feet in length, and a wicker shield covered in leather. For versatility in battle, they also carried a sagaris, a type of axe with a flat blade and a sharp point.

The Immortals had further protection from their breastplates. They are made up of small bronze plates over lapping one another, giving the appearance of serpent like scales.

As the Immortals marched towards the Greeks, their white loose felt caps, known as a tiara, are draped over their faces. They are thin enough to see through and protected their eyes from the dust being disrupted by ten thousand pairs of feet marching forward.

However, from where the Greeks were waiting at the middle gate, all ten thousand faces appear white and featureless.

'I don't think this is going to end well, I've heard many stories on how they can't be killed,' a Thespian soldier says nervously.

'I can promise you one thing,' – Leonidas says confidently, adjusting his helmet – 'we are going to test their name, Immortals. We shall see.'

The Immortals approach the Greeks and stop a few hundred yards from the Spartan phalanx. Little did they know Leonidas has a plan to lure them in, restricting their numbers further.

Leonidas has anticipated they would stop a few hundred yards out. The Immortals did this so their enemies could observe their huge numbers, weapons and featureless faces. An intimidation tactic.

Leonidas used this to his advantage ordering a feigning retreat.

'Fall back,' he orders.

The Greeks retreat deeper in to the pass, the Spartan follow until they are within the narrowest part of the pass, only fifteen meters across.

The Immortals take the bait.

'Charge!' the commanding Immortal orders, assuming the Greeks were retreating from fear of their reputation. They charge the Spartans head on.

At the point of contact the Immortals were far deeper in to the pass than Xerxes expected, vastly limiting their advantage of numbers.

The Spartans are not remotely intimidated, adrenaline flows throw their bodies, like a drug.

They release an almighty battle cry that would make Hades himself stand to attention.

Xerxes and the Immortals have now realised their fatal mistake, they have underestimated the Spartans.

The Immortals find themselves at the point of no return.

The Spartans get to work, swiftly chopping the Immortals down, one by one.

22

The morning of day two; bodies from the previous battle litter the ground. The Spartans had wiped out devastating numbers of Immortals, but not without losses of their own.

'Well, they weren't Immortal,' Tiro says, giving one of the corpse's a kick.

Leonidas smirks, 'Let's clear this area and dump their bodies two hundred yards in front. Force them to climb over their own comrades when they next attack.'

'You think they'll still attack us after annihilating their strongest soldiers?'

'I have no question in my mind Tiro, Xerxes won't want to leave us to regain our strength. He is relying on us fatiguing.'

'He's got a long wait, my King,' replies Aristodemus.

Noticing his eye injury isn't improving, Leonidas calls Aristodemus over for a closer look.

'I'm ok, my King, it's just a scratch.'

'That is not a scratch, my friend, it has become infected,' Leonidas says with a concerned look on his face.

His eye was swollen and partially closed, weeping a milky coloured substance that clearly irritated Aristodemus as he continued to rub it. His visibility was poor and Leonidas had concerns over the defense he could provide in their phalanx.

'There is no room for weakness in our phalanx Aristodemus.'

'Yes, my King, but we have lost several of our men and we could do with all the help we can get right now.'

Leonidas pauses momentarily to think, 'Ok, for now you can remain in formation. Keep your wits up.'

Later that morning, the Persian King was at camp massaging his temples. He was feeling stressed as the Greeks have already delayed him longer than expected.

Thinking of other ways left to break through their defense was irritating Xerxes beyond belief. He was certain his famous Immortals would have walked through the Greeks with ease. Again, Xerxes had gone against Demaratus's advice and underestimated the Spartans.

Xerxes called for Hydarnes, a commander within his army.

'You called for me?' Hydarnes asks, as he approaches the King.

'Yes, what do you suggest we do next?'

'I would send in the infantry again my King. The Greeks are surely feeling fatigued and they have lost many men,' Hydarnes confidently replies.

'Very well, send them in.'

Xerxes observed his infantrymen from his throne as they marched off towards the pass, adamant this would be the final approach on the Spartans.

Xerxes could see the number of Greeks was significantly less. However, their discipline in the phalanx remained solid and they did not show any sign of backing down.

Xerxes continued to observe as his infantry clashed with the Greeks. Chaos commenced; the Spartans had broken their phalanx and were now fighting one on one.

It was hard for Xerxes to see which side had the advantage watching from a distance.

A rush of excitement rushes through his body when he believes his infantry have started to defeat the tired Greeks. The feeling soon fades as he begins to notice waves of infantrymen fall by Spartan swords.

'What's going on over there?' Xerxes asks out loud in frustration.

Hydarnes, who is stood a short distance from Xerxes, becomes overwhelmed with anxiety as he observes his men failing and Xerxes becoming increasingly irritable.

It is not long before the Spartans and their allies have made easy work of the Persians.

Xerxes could hear the Spartan battle cry as it echoed through the pass. The sound of their confidence made Xerxes cringe and shudder in despair.

'Fuck, why won't the Greek bastards die already! Stop the assault and withdraw the remaining men,' shouts Xerxes, perplexed and not knowing what to do next.

'But my King,' replied Hydarnes.

'Dot it, do it now!' orders Xerxes, fearful the Spartans will embarrass him further.

The Spartans begin to notice the gradual withdrawal of the Persians. They continued to advance, slaying as many Persians as they could before the retreated.

Eventually, the Persians have retreated and the Spartans let out a roaring cheer as they waved the Persians goodbye.

'They've not had a good day,' Alec says, sniggering to himself as he sarcastically continues to wave goodbye.

'Rest now, I don't think we will be hearing from the Persians again just yet. Feast well and regain your strength,' Leonidas orders.

Despite nobody complaining, the Spartans were beginning to fatigue and were fighting on pure adrenaline and passion. Leonidas was well aware of this; it was only a matter of time before they would fall.

Leonidas kept his thoughts to himself; he was proud of his men and the sacrifice they are willing to make.

Later that day, Xerxes has spent much of his time pondering over what move to make next. The ships were making slow progress and the land army has been stuck at the pass for too long.

Just as Xerxes was about to admit to himself that he was all out of ideas, one of his servants approaches.

'My King, someone is here requesting to see you.'

'Leonidas?' replies Xerxes, hoping he was coming to surrender.

'No, my King.'

'Then I am not interested.'

'My King, he insists on seeing you and believes he can help you win your battle.'

'Really? What are you waiting for? Send him through then.'

The man approaches Xerxes. 'Bow to me and tell me why you have requested the attention of my ears.'

'My name is Ephialtes, my King,' he nervously says, looking down at the ground.

Ephialtes is a local goatherder who knows the area well. He is a lonely person who has little to no wealth of any kind, and he hopes Xerxes will change his fortune.

'Ephialtes, you better not be wasting my time. Continue.'

'I believe I can show you a way around the Greeks.'

Xerxes laughs loudly, 'Is that right? How so? I am unaware of such a way.' The King is intrigued by the man.

'Forgive me, my King. How will I be rewarded for such information?'

'I am Xerxes, King of Kings, I can get you anything you desire.'

'Ok, Very well. There is a narrow path that I can lead your men on, it will take you over the top of the pass and behind the Greeks.'

Xerxes smile reaches from ear to ear, 'Tell me, why a fellow Greek would betray his own nation, so easily?'

'I am in love with a Spartan girl called Ellas.'

Xerxes abruptly interrupts him, 'Ah, a woman. Let me guess, she doesn't love you back?'

Ephialtes silence confirms Xerxes prediction.

'Yes, my King, it appears I am not good enough for an educated woman within the Spartan society.'

Xerxes places his hands on his shoulders, 'I promise you; she will live to regret that decision. If you are right about this path, when I conquer all of Greece, I will march you through Sparta myself and make Ellas one of your many wives.

'One of my wives?'

'Yes, and any other woman you desire.'

Ephialtes was excited, it had been a long time since he had embraced a woman.

'And riches?' Hoping he wasn't pushing his luck.

'Endless amounts of gold and land.'

'Thank you, my King, thank you.'

'Show our savior around and let him feast. Hydarnes, gather what's left of the Immortals and other units. Prepare to advance under moonlit skies.'

That evening, Hydarnes gathers twenty thousand men from the remaining Immortals and the infantry. The evening is cool and clear and the moon casts a dim light across the pass. Hundreds of camp fires can be seen all along the coast casting large, long shadows of the camps occupants against the cliff faces.

Fortunately for the Persians, the plan is to advance through the mountain pass under heavy cover from the trees, surrounding the Greeks to prevent a retreat.

Ephialtes stands at the front of the twenty thousand Persians, Hydarnes gives him the nod of approval to lead the way.

Ephialtes has never felt such power and self-importance as the Persian army begins to follow his lead.

The path led east of the Persian camp along the steep ridge of Mount Anopaea, behind the cliffs that flanked the hot gates.

Ephialtes agreed he would lead Hydarnes and his men to where the path branched off, with one path leading to Phocis and the other down to the Malian Gulf at Alpenus, leading to the first town of Locris.

The path was hard to follow in such darkness. A few breaks in the tree lines allowed the moonlight to light up the path and avoid any protruding tree roots or broken ankles.

The Persians moved silently and slowly, but they had little time to waste. The majority of the Persians needed to cross over the mountain and be on the other side of the pass by dawn avoiding any opportunity for the Greeks to counterattack.

23

Dawn of day three; Ephialtes has led Hydarnes and his men to where the path branched off.

The Greeks guarding the path above Thermopylae hear a rustling in the bushes ahead.

'Who is that?' the Phocians ask in a panic.

There is no response and the rustling stops. As the Phocians approach, Ephialtes and Hydarnes suddenly appear.

The Phocians saw the large body of Persians following on from behind, it was now clear they were being outflanked.

Both parties are equally surprised to see each other and there was a sudden scramble to gather their weapons, hastily arming themselves.

Hugely outnumbered and assuming the Persians had come to attack them, the Phocians retreated to a nearby hill to make their stand for the pass.

'Fuck, Spartans!' Hydarnes says, fearful that the Phocians were the well-trained warriors he dreaded to face.

'No, they are not Spartans. They look like Phocians,' informs Ephialtes.

Hydarnes could not afford any further delays and orders his archers to send a volley of arrows towards the Phocians.

The arrows whistled through the air towards the Phocians who ran in fear of being hit, the majority taking arrows to their backs as they try to find cover.

The Phocians did not put up a fight and the Persians quickly bypassed them to continue their encirclement.

'Shit, that was close,' Ephialtes says, placing his hands-on top of his head in disbelief.

'Let's continue,' Hydarnes orders.

'My job is done; my agreement was to get you to the path where it branches off.

'I'm in charge out here, you stay with us until I say so,' Hydarnes demands.

Unbeknown to the Hydarnes, a Persian man known as Tyrrhastiadas was on his way to warn the Greeks. Tyrrhastiadas was a Persian captain and noble who took pity on the Greeks as he was married to a Greek woman.

Upon his arrival, he is met with reluctance. Spartan officers, escort him under watchful eye to Leonidas.

'Leonidas, I am Tyrrhastiadas. I must inform you the Phocians have not held the path on the ridge, you are being outflanked as we speak. You must retreat or surrender immediately!'

'Retreat, Surrender. Highly unlikely but thank you, you are dismissed,' replies Leonidas, nodding to his officers to escort him away.

The Greeks debate about remaining to fight or whether they should retreat. Leonidas, recalling the words of the Oracle, was committed to sacrificing his life in order to save Sparta.

'I won't force you to stay, if any of you want to leave then do so now. You will still have some time before we are completely surrounded,' he said to the Greeks.

Many of the Greeks took him up on his offer and fled, wishing the Spartans well.

Leonidas and his Spartans are left with approximately two thousand soldiers who are willing to stay behind to fight and die. The Thebans and Thespians wanted to stay to fight off the Persians for as long as possible to delay the invasion in to their cities.

'We are only a few hundred now, Leonidas. We fight with you to the very end, my King,' Demophilus says, as he commands his remaining Thespians to prepare for one last battle.

Leonidas returns a nod of gratitude.

The remaining four hundred Thebans join the ranks of the Thespians, eager to perform their last act of valour.

A short while after the Greeks retreat, Leonidas makes a request.

'Aristodemus and Eurytus, you are both severely injured. You are no good to me here. You must go back to Sparta and tell our story, let them know what happened here and that we made the ultimate sacrifice for Sparta, inspire new generations to do the same.'

'My King, please let us stay. We can still fight,' they both request simultaneously.

'We will be treated as cowards, my King,' says Eurytus.

'Agreed, we are better off dead, my King.'

Leonidas smiles, impressed with their loyalty. You are both nearly blind.'

'Yes, nearly, so let me fight until I am blind,' replies Aristodemus.

'I will miss your stubbornness my friend. Please do as I say. Remember us. Go tell the Spartans, passer-by, that here, by Spartan law, we lie.'

'As you wish, my King,' agreeing to return to Sparta.

'You must leave now, you do not have much time,' urges Leonidas.

They embrace the King, then reluctantly go on their way. It was not a comfortable feeling walking away from their comrades, it left a feeling of sickness in their stomach.

Moments later, the Persians advance towards the pass. Hydarnes forces begin to block their route of retreat, slaying the stragglers that did not leave quick enough.

Aristodemus and Eurytus would not have an easy escape, they would have to navigate their way through the pass without being seen.

Leonidas took a deep breath, his final thoughts going in to battle are that of Gorgo and Pleistarchus.

The Spartans and remaining Greeks clash with the Persians in a ferocious one on one battle, the Greeks making easy work of the Persians.

The Spartan attack was so aggressive there were few Persians that could handle such skill. Arms and legs are removed so swiftly, moments pass before the recipient even realises what has happened.

Leonidas's battle cry can be heard above anyone else's, to the Persians he seems possessed. To the Greeks and his fellow Spartans, he is an inspirational force of nature that's providing them with the motivation to keep fighting.

Cutting his way through crowds of Persians, they fall at his feet with every strike of his sword. He shows no signs of slowing down, determined to kill as many as he can before he is imminently struck down.

Xerxes sent his two brothers in to battle, Abrocomes and Hyperanthes, at their own request. They had hopes they could claim to be the ones who strike down the Spartan King.

Leonidas is surrounded, as quickly as he kills one Persian, another replaces the void.

Demophilus makes a heroic attempt to make his way to Leonidas to provide some support. He is quickly overwhelmed by a dozen Persian swords from all angles. As blood discharges from his mouth, he spits in the face of a Persian as a final act of defiance.

Terrified by the display Leonidas is demonstrating, Abrocomes musters up the courage to strike at him. His feeble attempt fails miserably as Leonidas pivots perfectly on the balls of his feet, using his body weight to shunt Abrocomes out of the way, slicing his sword across his belly.

Abrocomes lets out a horrific scream as his guts spill out in to his hands.

Outraged by his sibling's death, Hyperanthes pulls out a spear lodged in a Persian Corpse. Barging through the Persians he thrusts the spear through Leonidas's shoulder.

Unphased, Leonidas roars in the face of Hyperanthes. Despite the pain he is suffering, he refuses to show it.

He uses his sword to cut through the shaft of the spear, eliminating the advantage of length. Still dangerous, a now sluggish Leonidas swings recklessly with the use of one arm. He throws his sword forward, using every part of his being to muster up the strength. The sword slams in to Hyperanthes's sternum with a thud, killing him instantly.

'My King!' shouts Tiro, simultaneously slaying three Persians with ease.

A Persian Horseman approaches Tiro, who he immediately immobilises by thrusting his spear in to the Horseman's neck, throwing him off the horse.

Tiro leaps on to the horse in an attempt to get to Leonidas faster.

The majority of Persians were still too afraid to approach Leonidas. Struggling to finish him off, an archer fires two arrows in to his chest, making him fall to his knees.

'No!' Tiro cries out, slashing at the Persians as he gallops by.

Before he can reach the King, another Persian Horseman clashes in to Tiro, slashing his sword upwards. Tiro's face is split from his cheek and up across his nose and forehead.

Tiro slumps forward, his blood spilling down the neck of the horse. Startled, the horse bolts from battlefield with Tiro's limp body remaining on the horse.

Alec notices the bloodstained horse run out of the battle with his comrade's body slumped over it.

The remaining Spartans have gathered around to protect Leonidas as he still remains on his knees, gasping for air.

Alec joins the scuffle, ending the Persians with his two blades. His energy taking the Persians by surprise, as if he is fresh in to battle.

'Retrieve the King,' Alec demands, fighting off the Persians while attempting to lift the King to his feet.

The Spartans eventually gathered to Kolonos hill to gain some advantage of higher ground. However, with Hydarnes now approaching, the Spartans must make their last stand, together.

Leonidas, now laying on his back, wheezes for air. From the top of Kolonos hill he tilts his head to observe the battleground.

Carnage, chaos and destruction, exactly what Leonidas wanted to create. Dead Persians as far as the eyes can see, the ocean washing in waves of blood as the bodies of Persians tumble in the tide.

Leonidas's breathing becomes shallower by the minute, he reminisces on the final moments with his family. Suddenly, he attempts to focus on a blurry image that has appeared before him. As it becomes clearer, Leonidas spots the white owl, '*Tuto.*' A sign that has appeared consistently throughout pivotal moments in his life. He believes this to be reassurance from the Gods, a final message of hope, that Greece will prevail and he can die knowing his contribution was crucial for its survival.

Leonidas knows this to be the last time he will see the Gods sign, one that has helped him be guided by his instincts.

A final thought goes through his mind, *'Gorgo, my Queen, my love.'*

As the white owl comes closer, its white feathers become brighter, until Leonidas see's nothing but a brilliant white light.

Alec places his hand on Leonidas's chest, his wheezing has stopped, his eyes are open but they are vacant. The King is dead.

Xerxes approaches the battleground, knowing the Spartans are surrounded. Tearing down part of the Greek wall, Xerxes spots his dead brothers.

Pausing for a moment, he orders his commanders to lash the archers in to place with their whips. Xerxes orders his men to rain arrows on the Spartans, until every single one is dead.

The Spartans are now surrounded by hundreds of archers, there is nowhere for them to go. They resist for as long as they can with their swords, if they had them. If not, with their fists, taking down Persians and biting through their necks with their teeth.

Eventually, more Persians make it over the ruins of the wall and are closing in from all directions, finally overwhelming the Spartans.

Alec kneels beside Leonidas, his friend. Cradling his head, he shuts Leonidas's eyes.

Suddenly, he hears the sound of hundreds of bowstrings releasing their arrows. Alec leans in further over Leonidas's body and shuts his eyes, embracing his last few seconds of life. The arrows settle, finding their targets. The Spartans have fallen, but they have fallen for Sparta. A death worth living for.

24

After the battle, Xerxes approaches Kolonos hill. The King, usually respectful to those who have perished in battle, makes the decision to dismember Leonidas.

Xerxes removes Leonidas's head and orders his trunk to be affixed to a cross, along with all the other Spartans. This was an act of anger; Xerxes knew Leonidas had managed to achieve what he needed to. Delay his armies and waste his resources, and in the process both his siblings were killed.

Xerxes now needed to regroup his army and proceed with his mission of invading Greece.

A short distance from Thermopylae, Aristodemus and Eurytus have miraculously avoided capture. They have both noticed the distant rumbles from the battle have since faded.

'Can you hear anything anymore, Aristodemus?'

Aristodemus pauses for a moment to listen, 'No, it seems the battle might be over.'

'I can't do it, brother.'

'Can't do what, Eurytus?'

'Return to Sparta, we will be cowards. Our lives will not be worth living!'

'Calm yourself down, we owe it to our comrades. We made a promise to our King to make sure they are remembered. I would gladly be labelled a coward knowing I have obeyed my orders until the end.'

'Bollocks, I'm sorry Aristodemus I just can't do it.' Eurytus turns around and runs back towards Thermopylae.

'You can barely see where you're going!'

Eurytus continues to run and doesn't look back. That was the last time Aristodemus would ever see him.

For Aristodemus, orders are orders, regardless of the consequences. He was determined to make it back to Sparta.

The weather had turned against him. Heavy rain storms had moved in from the coast prolonging his journey back to Sparta.

His eye was not getting any better. He stares in to the rain to help clean and sooth the eye, trying not to touch it. Unfortunately, the infection has already taken hold and he was now rendered permanently blind in his eye.

His journey home was tough, his body still ached from the previous days of fighting, he had several deep wounds from the Persian attacks.

Several days later, Aristodemus arrives on the outskirts of Sparta. He stops in his tracks as he approaches a tree with a Spartan hanging at the end of a rope. Aristodemus knows him as Pantites. It appears he has not been dead long.

Aristodemus releases the rope and lowers Pantites to the ground.

As he enters the city, it doesn't take long before he starts causing a stir. Being the only Spartan to return from Thermopylae, people begin to whisper among themselves.

'Look, a Trembler!' shouts a citizen.

Aristodemus looks around, citizens are shaking their heads in disgrace. He quickly makes his way to Leonidas's house to address Gorgo.

Gorgo is stunned to see him. 'You are the last person I expected to see.'

His presence confirms Leonidas is dead and she would soon have to break the news to Pleistarchus.

'My Queen, I'm sorry.'

'Do not apologise, Leonidas sent you back, didn't he?'

'Yes, he sent me back to tell his story because of this injury,' he says, pointing to his eye injury.

Gorgo observes the eye, 'Looks nasty, we'll get that treated for you.'

'It's unlikely anyone is going to want to treat a trembler, my lady.'

'C'mon Aristodemus, those that know you will always know you were loyal to Leonidas.'

'We'll see, my lady. I think the council will have a bit more to say on the matter.'

'I will arrange an immediate meeting at the Gerousia. This will give you an opportunity to pass the message and clear things up.'

'Yes, my lady.'

'After that, you must rest,' insists Gorgo.

'What happened to Pantites?' He asks, with a puzzled look on his face.

'Ah yes, I heard about him, he committed suicide. He received a lot of grief. Leonidas sent him to recruit reinforcements before they left, and then rendezvous at Thermopylae.'

Aristodemus looked confused, 'I don't remember seeing him at Thermopylae.'

'That's because he didn't go. After failing to recruit allies, he didn't want to attend Thermopylae empty handed. After it was discovered, he hung himself. The council insisted his body remained there for the crows,' explains Gorgo.

'Right, I see,' says Aristodemus, struggling to come to terms with his own survival.

Gorgo holds Aristodemus by the arms, 'Your circumstances are completely different, you are following orders of the King.'

That afternoon, Gorgo and Aristodemus make their way to the Gerousia. By now, word had got around the city that a Trembler had returned from Thermopylae.

As Aristodemus makes his way to the Gerousia, citizens begin to heckle and shout abuse. Some throwing objects at him in disgust.

'Fuck off, Trembler!'

'You're no Spartan!'

'You have no place here anymore!'

Aristodemus was incredibly thick skinned. He had been through a lot and knew he was doing what his King had asked of him. As long as he knew the truth, that's all that mattered to him. Still, he couldn't help but question how he would ever fit back in to society.

At the Gerousia, Cleombrotus approaches Aristodemus and embraces him.

'Gorgo has already informed me what happened,' says Cleombrotus.

'Thank you.'

There was already a heated debate within the Gerousia, some for and some against Aristodemus returning to Sparta. As he walks in to the Gerousia, everyone in attendance becomes silent.

'So, the rumours are true, Spartan,' Lycurgus says, not quite believing he has survived.

Some of the elders heckle Aristodemus, labelling him a disgrace, before he has even had the chance to speak.

'Let him speak!' shouts Lycurgus.

'The floor is yours, Spartan,' says Gorgo, directing him to address the council.

'I know my presence here disappoints you. However, if being labelled a trembler for the rest of my life means I still remain loyal to my King, so be it.'

The council remains silent. 'Carry on,' says Lycurgus, encouraging Aristodemus to continue.

'The truth is known between Leonidas and I, that's how I know I can live with myself and whatever label I am given.'

Aristodemus continues telling their heroic story of Thermopylae in great detail, up until the point he was ordered to leave.

Aristodemus's story telling of Spartan courage gripped the council from start to finish. After delivering Leonidas's message, Aristodemus emphasises the purpose of his return.

'His message was simple, Remember us.'

By the time Aristodemus has finished, he has turned the tide in his favour.

Lycurgus approaches the floor, 'Based on your account of events, and the fact we are in no position to prove otherwise, you shall remain a Spartan citizen and keep your place within our army. Does anybody object?'

The council agrees with the decision, but Aristodemus knows he will still have to prove himself, especially within the phalanx of the Spartan army.

'Furthermore, now we know Xerxes resources and that he relies on sheer volume, rather than tactics and skill. We can plan accordingly for his imminent attack,' suggests Lycurgus.

Gorgo takes Aristodemus by the hand, 'It'll take people time to come around to the truth. For now, we need to get that eye sorted out.

'Yes, my lady,' he replies, feeling a weight lifted from his shoulders.

The council dismiss and Aristodemus leaves to get his eye treated.

A moment later, as Aristodemus is leaving, Gorgo runs over to him.

'Aristodemus, I have one question.'

'Yes, my lady, anything.'

'Will I ever get him back?'

'Honestly, my lady, I don't know.'

Gorgo nods her head, saddened that she may never retrieve Leonidas's remains.

'I wonder how he faced his final moments.'

'Unfortunately, I wasn't there. However, I do know he would have fought until his very last breath,' – Aristodemus places his hand affectionately around her arm – 'Remember how he lived and know, he died in war, the greatest honour for any Spartan.'

'Thank you, Aristodemus,' replies Gorgo. A single tear escapes down her cheek, she quickly wipes it away not wanting to show any signs of weakness.

'You will have your vengeance, as will Sparta, my lady.'

'I hope so, I truly hope so.'

'The battle was lost, but the war is not over.'

25

Three months pass. Deep within the mountains of the Opuntian Locris region, north east of the Phocis area of central Greece and home of the mythical hero Ajax of the Trojan war, there is a Locrian farmer called Theodore and his wife, Calisto, going about their daily lives.

Winter has set in, the snowfall has been consistent for several weeks, restricting access on or off of the mountain.

The couple are out of the way of trouble and are relatively self-sustainable. However, they are aware of the Persian invasion and the battle of Thermopylae that took place several months previously, to the north of Phocis near Epicnemidian Locris.

As they are isolated from the general population, they are able to successfully hide a secret.

'How much longer do you think we can carry on doing this?' asks Calisto, with a concerned look on her face.

'He is getting stronger, my love.'

Calisto is nursing a man back to health that Theodore brought home one day, finding him on a random mountain path three months previously.

The man was mortally wounded, and has not been fully coherent since being taken care of.

His beard and hair have become excessively long.

The couple have struggled to keep him fed, waiting for moments where he has been partially conscious to quickly feed him a mouthful of stew, before slipping back in to unconsciousness.

As a result, the man looks emaciated and with the harsher winter weather yet to come, they are not sure the man will pull through, yet they persevere.

Calisto has spent much of her time nursing the man, while Theodore is out farming.

'Has he woken up at all, Calisto?' asks Theodore, returning home.

'No, but his eye lids keep twitching and he has been having horrific nightmares and cold sweats, he shouted something about a King.'

Theodore folds his arms and takes a minute to observe the man, 'He's a fighter, I'll give him that.'

'Yes, providing he doesn't suffer with another fever like the one he had a few weeks ago, that would finish him off,' Calisto says, wiping the man's brow with a damp cloth.

'Keep up the good work, my love. You are doing a great job.'

'I just wish we knew who he was.'

'You and me both Calisto. You and me both.'

Theodore kneels down, pulling out a large wooden trunk from under the bed. He opens it up to reveal the man's battle-damaged amour. He runs his fingers over the surface of the breastplate, it was clear just from observing the amour this man has been through hell.

'I've seen armour like this before, Calisto.'

'From a Greek soldier, that's what you originally thought.'

Theodore nods his head in agreement, 'Yes, definitely Greek, but I have been giving it more thought. Look at this, I think this is his cloak.'

'And?' responds Calisto, waiting for Theodore to elaborate.

'This isn't just Greek armour, this is Spartan armour.'

'You think he's a Spartan?'

'Yes, it makes sense, don't you think? The battle of Thermopylae was just north of here, around the same period of time I came across him.'

'That doesn't explain why you found him so far from Thermopylae, assuming that's where he came from. You know as well as the rest of Greece, Spartans do not abandon their comrades.'

Suddenly, the man starts coughing violently. He coughs up a small amount of blood that Calisto wipes away from his chin. She rolls him over on to his side and firmly pats his back.

'That's not a good sign,' a concerned Theodore says.

'I'm tired, my love. I can't do any more for him, it's up to him now,' an exhausted Calisto replies, leaving the house to get some fresh air.

Several more day's pass, Calisto is attending to the man as usual. She bathes him with a warm damp cloth. As she wipes down his arm, the man grabs her hand and attempts to speak.

'Theodore, come quick!'

Theodore runs in from outside where he was collecting logs for the fire.

'What's wrong?'

'He grabbed my hand and he is trying to say something, I can't make out what he is whispering.'

Theodore leans over the man, looking down his chest he places his ear next to his mouth.

'What is he saying?'

'He asked if he was dead.'

'Oh, he didn't say anything else?'

The man's breathing was raspy. Theodore fetches a small cup of water and pours small amounts in to the man's mouth.

The man splutters and coughs, then partially opens his eyes.

'Hello, can you hear me?' asks Theodore.

The man slowly nods his head.

'You are not dead, you are safe. My name is Theodore and this is my wife, Calisto.'

The man's eyes roll back in to his head and he falls back in to a deep state of sleep.

As the evening draws in, it's been several hours since the man spoke and opened his eyes. Theodore and Calisto are eating their supper; the conversation is at a minimum.

They hear a groan coming from the man, both getting up as quickly as they can, they attend to him; this time his eyes are wide open. They say nothing and wait for the man to talk in his own time.

He attempts to sit up, oblivious to his diminished strength.

Theodore and Calisto take an arm each and sit the man up, making sure he is comfortable.

His head feels heavy, slouching over under his own weight. Noticing his emaciated body, he winces at the sight of himself.

'Where am I? I need to go,' says the man, in a hurry to leave.

'You don't have the strength to hold your head up, let alone walk out of here.'

'I agree, please listen to my wife, she has been nursing you for three months.'

'Three months!' the man says, followed by a coughing fit.

'It's been touch and go for you on more than one occasion, my friend,' Theodore tells him.

'It's true, you have suffered terrible fevers, infections and nightmares, often calling out to your King.'

'Who is your King? What happened to you?' asks Theodore, inpatient for answers.

The man suffers from a painful headache, causing him to press his hand against his temple.

Flashbacks taunt his mind, displaying memories of Spartans and Persians being slaughtered.

He lays back down, exhausted at the thought of wanting to stand up.

'Why am I here? Where am I?' the man curiously asks, disorientated and unable to process how much time has passed.

'This is our farm, in the mountains of the Opuntian Locris region. My husband found you on the mountain path, he thought you were dead.'

'I'd be better off dead, you should have left me there,' the man replies.

'Well, you were badly wounded. No soldier deserves to be left to die.'

'Did you find me with anything else?'

'No, you had no weapons on you. Although, there were horse prints in the mud.'

'Horse prints?'

'Yes, is it possible you came on horseback? You were in no state to ride though, so maybe someone dumped you there,' suggests Theodore, searching for answers.

'I'm tired,' the man replies, laying back down to sleep.

Calisto puts her hand on his forehead, 'Rest now, we will talk more tomorrow.'

The next morning, Theodore hasn't slept well after listening to the man suffer from nightmares for the majority of the night. The man is out of his bed and standing, albeit unsteady.

'Steady now, you haven't used those legs for some time,' Theodore says, reminds him.

The man's wounds have healed relatively well, but it will take some time to regain his strength. His legs are weak and suffering with bed sores.

'Are you hungry? You need to build your strength,' asks Calisto.

'You won't get off this mountain in this weather and in your condition. Stay with us until you regain your strength,' insists Theodore.

The man nods gently, 'Very well.'

Theodore and Calisto look at one another, relieved he is in agreement to stay.

The man didn't say much for the rest of the day, until unprompted, he speaks.

'I am a Spartan.'

'I knew it!'

'Were you at Thermopylae?' asks Calisto.

'Yes, I remember being at the pass, but I do not remember how I ended up here.'

The Spartan thought long and hard, all it did was create further headaches and unanswered questions.

'My comrades,' the Spartan whispers to himself.

'Maybe I can help fill in some of the gaps, my friend? Word travelled around the land quickly that the Spartans fought to the last man standing, delaying Xerxes long enough for ally states to evacuate.'

'The last man?' says the Spartan.

'Yes, I'm afraid all the Spartans were killed in the battle. However, it would appear this is untrue,' says Theodore, cracking a smile.

The Spartan sighs, disappointed at the news, disappointed further that he has not perished with them.

'What happened to Xerxes?'

'He's progressing quickly through Greece. The last I heard he had conquered the city of Athens.'

'Athens has fallen?'

'Yes, quite literally. Xerxes burnt it to the ground. Fortunately, you and the Greeks delayed Xerxes long enough for the citizens to abandon the city.'

The Spartan touches his face, feeling the heavy scarring from his wounds. 'I remember being struck, then everything went black. I assumed I had met my end in battle, alongside my brothers.'

The Spartan falls in to a state of day dream, starring in to the crackling fire as Theodore loads it with more logs.

'Spartan,' calls Calisto, requesting his attention.

'Yes.'

'What is your name?'

Theodore stops what he is doing, wondering to himself why he hasn't asked the same question yet. There is a prolonged moment of silence.

'My name?'

'Yes, your name, what is it?'

'My name. . .my name is Tiro, of Messene, son of Orien.

'Well, it's officially nice to meet you, Tiro of Messene,' says Calisto.

A few weeks later, Tiro has gained weight and has a strong appetite, building his strength each day. To keep himself active he has helped out Theodore and Calisto as much as he can on the farm. However, he has a burning desire to return to Sparta.

Unsure how they will react to his survival, he is keen to fall back in to the Spartan phalanx.

The snow has significantly thawed and the mountain paths are now accessible. The time has come for Tiro to leave.

Calisto hands him enough supplies for his journey back.

'Thank you, both, for what you have done. I have come to the conclusion the Gods sent me to you for a reason. There is a purpose to my journey.'

'You are welcome, Tiro. Goodbye,' says an emotional Calisto, embracing Tiro, kissing his cheek.

'What is that purpose, Tiro?' asks Theodore, putting his arm out as a gesture to embrace arms.

'Vengeance,' Tiro says, firmly embracing Theodore's arm with a smile.

Printed in Great Britain
by Amazon